Perkin
Perkins, Victoria.
Reeves' island /
$9.00   on1082870274

3 4028 10040 0408
HARRIS COUNTY PUBLIC LIBRARY

Y0-AVB-459

DISCARD

Copyright 2014 Victoria Perkins

All Scripture is from the public domain pdf found at

http://WorldEnglishBible.org.

As always, my family deserves acknowledgement
and thanks for their unending support.

To the students, staff and faculty of the real WCS.
From the moment the doors opened until the day they closed,
WCS left its mark on each person who entered the building.
Though WCS is no longer in operation
its legacy lives on in each life that it touched.

Preface

Reeves' Island has been through more incarnations than anything I've ever written. When I first came up with the idea, I was twelve years-old, a seventh grader at Warren Christian School, and looking to find a place. As the years passed and my writing matured, I took another pass. Since the first draft had been written in 19*ahem* and I was looking at it years later, I had to take into account technological changes. I also found that the characters were much more hopeful that I would have made them had I written the original story as an adult. I considered changing it, but ultimately decided against it. In the end, I like that Arisa and Will and the others don't succumb to the darkness that other literary characters do. Maybe it's a bit naïve, but the twelve year-old inside me thinks that's okay.

REEVES' ISLAND

Chapter One

"Tony!" A young woman called out across the crowded hallway. She quickly made her way over to her seventeen year-old boyfriend and asked if he'd heard the news.

Tony Vumeccelli shook his head, looking down at his eighteen year-old girlfriend. His hazel eyes sparkled as he reached out and took her hand, ignoring Wycliffe Christian School's policy about 'public displays of affection.'

"I guess the school's sending some younger kids, like junior high and freshmen, to some kind of special workshop-type camp somewhere. It's a week long and any upperclassman who goes gets bonus points in all their classes."

"Did you already sign up?" Tony ran his free hand through his thick black hair.

"You know I wouldn't do that without you. What would be fun about going all by myself?" Reese looked up at Tony, light blue eyes wide. "I might need a strong handsome man to protect me from all of those rowdy kids." She paused and grinned. "But I suppose I could settle for you."

"Thanks." Tony spoke sarcastically, but without malice. He smiled. "It sounds like a trip we can't afford to pass up." Tony pulled Reese to him and slipped an arm around her shoulder, giving her a quick hug.

"Watch the PDA, Reese!" Fellow cheerleader Jessica Chapman called out as she passed the couple.

Reese stuck out her tongue at her friend as Tony reached for her hand once more. "We're supposed to see Mrs. McKennedy if we want to go."

"Well then, let's go."

The couple made their way down the hall and turned right when the hallway ended. They passed one classroom and then walked through a doorway into the medium-sized classroom. They made their way through the neat rows of chairs and desks as they walked toward the teacher's desk. Standing at the back of the room with Mrs. McKennedy were two of Tony and Reese's friends.

"Hey, Arisa, Cassidy." Reese greeted the younger girls with a pleasant smile and a nod.

"Hi, Reese." Sixteen year-old Arisa McDonald smiled, her bright blue eyes lighting up when she saw her friends. She absently tucked a strand of golden blond hair behind her ear and nodded at Reese and then at Tony. "Hey, Tony."

"Hey, girls." Tony said, smiling at his longtime friend and then turning his grin towards the dark-eyed girl at Arisa's side. Cassidy Chapman had been friends with Arisa for years, and when Tony began fifth grade at Wycliffe Christian School, the girls had taken pity on the new kid and shown him around. Reese came three years later. Arisa and Cassidy had already known her, having met Reese at church camp the year before, and they were more than happy to introduce her to their friend. Tony and Reese began dating four months later and had been together ever since, despite both of their parents' strong disapproval of the relationship. They had been voted "Cutest Couple" two years in a row and were looking at a third time with the title. They had also made plans to attend Wycliffe University, much to the dismay of both sets of parents who'd been hoping the pair would split after graduation.

Arisa turned her attention back to the petite, dark-haired teacher behind the desk. "When will you know if it's definite?"

Mrs. McKennedy was one of the most well liked teachers in the school. She had been at the school for almost ten years – a surprise to first time families who often thought she was still in her mid-twenties – and was among the most respected teachers at WCS. Many of the students counted the teacher among their friends and often went to her for spiritual guidance or any other type of advice they needed.

"Wait a minute," Tony interrupted, "are you talking about going to that camp thing?"

"I already have more than enough teachers signed up to go,

but the camp wants at least four student counselors. It's some type of peer-mentoring program."

"And I just had to back out." Cassidy explained. "Nora has a riding competition on Tuesday and the whole family's going."

"That means we only have Arisa and a new junior." Mrs. McKennedy tucked a curl behind her ear.

Arisa gave the teacher a questioning look.

"Will Johnson. His brother and sister are going."

Arisa nodded, recalling the shy new student. He seemed nice enough, but the past two weeks had been too busy for her to do more than say a few words here and there. He sat behind her in Miss. Micheals' advanced English class, but she and Cassidy spent most of their free class time working on the school paper. She made a mental note to talk to him later that day.

"Reese and I were just coming to sign up." Tony gave the teacher a charming smile. "Does that mean we can go?"

"Yes, thank you both." Mrs. McKennedy handed some forms to Tony and Reese who filled them out as she continued to talk. "I'd have hated to cancel the trip. My nephew always loved going. It's really quite an honor for some of these kids to be chosen. Camp Ventner only looks at the very best students in seventh through ninth grade and this was the first year the camp has ever considered students from our school."

"What exactly do the kids do there?" Tony asked.

"Camp Ventner offers advanced classes in various areas. Science, English, math, foreign languages, music. They have some of the best people in each field come to the camp and teach. It's a wonderful opportunity for these kids."

"Sounds great, Mrs. McKennedy. Here you are." Tony handed his form to Mrs. McKennedy while pocketing the one that needed his parents' signature.

Reese handed both of her papers to Mrs. McKennedy after giving Tony a self-satisfied smile. She enjoyed being a few months older than Tony, giving her the ability to sign her own permission slips.

"Thank you. You're leaving Monday morning. Make sure you're here at eight so the bus can leave before nine." Mrs. McKennedy looked over the forms she held. "And make sure you bring the permission slip back or you can't go."

The four high school students left the classroom together, three of them talking with eager anticipation of all the fun they would be having while Cassidy glumly listened. Her friends would be ready for anything, any adventure. Nothing could surprise them. Or so they thought.

*　*　*

"Don't worry, Mom, everything's going to be fine." Arisa carried her suitcase down the stairs as quietly as she could, not wanting to wake her still-sleeping siblings. "Mrs. McKennedy hired a bus to take us to the airport where the school's rented a private plane to take us to the island where Camp Ventner is. It's off the coast of Florida, I think. I'm not sure exactly where but I know we'll be flying over the ocean for at least forty minutes, so I guess it'll be pretty far away."

Mrs. McDonald suppressed a smile at her daughter's chattered assurances. While Arisa was normally a talkative child, it was rare to see her so energetic early in the morning. Usually Arisa didn't fully wake up until well after noon. She scheduled her classes every year with that in mind, making sure she had her easiest classes first thing.

Arisa continued without noticing her mother's amusement. "It's some ritzy island thing, not like church camp or the campgrounds we go to. And we have four teachers coming with us. The student counselors are in charge for mentoring and all that stuff, but any real problems go to the adults."

"What are you worried about, Mom?" Arisa's fourteen year-old sister, Twila, came into the living room and set down her suitcase next to her sleeping bag. "Nothing's going to happen." Twila picked up her pocketknife, a spool of thread and a tennis ball from on top of the microwave. While she waited for her mother to find her car keys, she began to juggle the three items, a trick she'd learned over the summer.

"I don't know why I'm so concerned." Mrs. McDonald shook her head as she pulled her keys from her cluttered purse. "I'm sure everything's going to be fine."

Twila tossed the ball and the thread onto a nearby chair and slipped the knife into her pocket. She picked up her things and followed her mother and Arisa outside and down the front steps to where the family mini van was waiting. The girls packed their things in the back of the van and then walked around front to get inside.

"I just have a really bad feeling about this. Promise me you two will be careful." Mrs. McDonald climbed into the driver's seat.

Arisa didn't like the uneasy look on her mother's face. Her mother was normally easy-going and trusted her oldest two implicitly. Even when they'd gone on a mission's trip over the summer, she hadn't acted this concerned – and that had been to Uganda.

"We promise, Mom." Twila said, climbing to the very back of the van. After she sat down, she pulled her thick, reddish-blond hair back into a ponytail. "But, I still think you're getting yourself all upset for nothing."

"She's right, Mom." Arisa assured her mother as she climbed into the passenger side of the van. Her mother's apprehension was starting to make her nervous. "There's nothing for you to worry about. What's the worst that could happen?"

"You're probably right, girls." Mrs. McDonald started the vehicle as the girls fastened their seatbelts. "Okay, now, we have to pick up that new family, the Johnsons, right? There are three of them?"

Arisa nodded. "Yeah, their car broke down Saturday morning. Will said they live on Siege Street, behind Living Waters."

*　　*　　*

"Will, be sure to take care of Candece and Ryan." Leesa Johnson pulled her fifteen year-old son aside.

"Don't worry, Mom." Will reassured his mother for the third time in the past hour. He carefully hid the grin that wanted to escape. His mom was great, even if she did tend to get a little overprotective of his younger brother and sister. When she'd gotten the notice that Candece and Ryan had been chosen to attend Camp Ventner, she'd been thrilled, but anxiety hadn't been far behind. She understood that her kids needed some freedom, but she never enjoyed being away from them. Will's blue-green eyes, so similar to his mother's, danced with excitement. "Candece and Ryan are going to be fine. They'll have a great time at Camp Ventner. We'll be back on Thursday. Everything will be fine."

"Are you sure you'll be okay?" Mrs. Johnson looked across the living room to where Will's two younger siblings sat on their rolled-up sleeping bags, watching out the window for their ride. Her forehead furrowed as she watched the pair for a few seconds before turning back to her eldest child.

"You worry too much, Mom." Will brushed impatiently at his shaggy blond hair. He sighed as he remembered he'd forgotten to get it cut before leaving. He didn't usually like his hair this long, but it would have to wait. He knew by the time he returned on Thursday it would be past his collar in the back. "It'll be good for us to get out of the house for a while and really get to know the kids in our school. We've been here for two months and don't know anyone very well. Don't you want

Candece and Ryan to make new friends?"

"Of course I do." Mrs. Johnson said with a sigh. She then looked directly at Will. "I want you to make friends, too." She hugged Will and then walked over to give Candece and Ryan hugs. Will glanced out of the window just as a mini van pulled in the driveway.

"Come on, Candece, Ryan. The McDonalds are here." Will picked up his backpack and pulled it over his shoulder. He took the suitcase from his thirteen year-old sister and carried it, along with his sleeping bag, out to the van as Ryan followed him with his own luggage, leaving the two remaining sleeping bags for Candece to carry.

*   *   *

"Good-bye! Have fun! Be good! Be careful!" Mrs. Johnson stood at the front door of her house, waving until the van pulled out of the driveway. As the vehicle disappeared down the road, Mrs. Johnson went back into the house and sank down in the nearest chair. Unable to shake the heavy feeling surrounding her, she prayed. "Dear Lord, please protect them. Watch over my children."

*   *   *

Will slid into the seat behind the passenger seat while Candece and Ryan moved to the back of the van. Twila smiled and instantly struck up a conversation. When Candece and Ryan found out Twila also liked their favorite band, shyness evaporated and they began to chatter about their favorite songs on the latest album.

Arisa glanced over at Will. "Looking forward to this?"

Will smiled shyly. "Yeah. It'll be good for Candece and Ryan to get to know some of their classmates."

"What are they going for?" Arisa caught her mother watching her in the rearview mirror. Mrs. McDonald smiled and turned her attention back to the road.

"Ryan for science and Candece for music. What about Twila?"

"Film. She's wanted to be a director from the time she was little. Always tried to make movies out of the books she'd read. Probably will end up some Hollywood big shot."

"Did you go to this camp when you were younger?"

Arisa shook her head. "They didn't offer it till this year. I wouldn't have made it anyway."

"Somehow, I doubt that." Will's cheeks reddened.

Arisa tried to put the young man at ease. "Did you have camps like this where you were from?"

Will shook his head. "No, but we always went to church camp every summer."

"Me too." Arisa latched onto the common experience. "What did you guys do?"

Will visibly relaxed as he began to tell Arisa about the church camps he'd enjoyed so much and how much he'd missed them this summer since his family had moved.

*   *   *

Tony checked his hair in the rearview mirror before getting out of his expensive European car. He walked up to the palatial three-story building Reese called home and rang the doorbell. The butler answered the door after only a few seconds.

"Miss. Reese will be out in a moment. Charles will bring out her luggage momentarily." The butler said curtly. After a pause, he reluctantly added, "You can wait in here, if you would like."

Tony smiled and walked past the older man into the front living room. He grinned as the butler scowled at him. Tony knew both Mr. and Mrs. Burnett were working at the moment. He knew this because his parents, both lawyers, had recently won a two-year-long case against the hospital, costing the administration several million dollars – and accidentally giving him full knowledge of the Burnetts' surgical rotations. Besides this obvious familial problem with him, the fact that Tony came from a long line of Catholic Italians with too close a connection to some unsavory families did little to increase his stature in the eyes of the proud Protestant Anglo-Saxon family to which Reese belonged. Even though he and his parents belonged to a local non-denominational Protestant church, the Burnetts refused to acknowledge Tony as a worthy candidate to spend time with their daughter in any capacity.

"Good morning, Tony!"

Tony smiled as Reese waltzed down the stairs. Tony greeted her with a hug and a quick kiss on the cheek, ignoring the glare from the butler.

"Are you ready to have some fun?"

Tony winked. "Let's go or we'll be late."

"Miss. Reese, your parents wanted me to make sure you had everything you needed." A maid came down the stairs. She glanced at Tony, not bothering to hide her disdain. She turned towards Reese.

"I do, Raquel." Reese took Tony's hand in her own. "Tell Daddy and Mommy I took next week's allowance just in case I need it."

"Yes, Miss. Reese." Raquel said. "Charles has already taken your things out to Mr. Vumeccelli's car. We will see you on Thursday, then."

"Until Thursday, Raquel. Tell Mommy and Daddy I love them." Reese followed Tony outside without even glancing back to see if the maid had heard her.

*   *   *

"How many suitcases do you need for a week?" Arisa asked. She laughed good-naturedly as Reese struggled to carry four suitcases through the single doorway. She opened the second door and held it.

Once inside, Reese stopped, setting down her suitcases with a thud. She smiled and took a deep breath before answering Arisa's half-joking question. "You have to be prepared for everything. It could be hot, or cold, or raining or you could rip something or..." Reese was caught up in reciting her list of weather conditions and catastrophes until Arisa politely interrupted her.

"Sorry, I don't mean to be rude, but I have to go talk to Mrs. McKennedy before we leave." Arisa excused herself and let the door swing shut behind her. She walked across the parking lot to where the bus waited. As she'd expected, Mrs. McKennedy was waiting next to it, clipboard in hand.

"Mrs. McKennedy." Arisa tapped the teacher on the shoulder. "Twila said you wanted to see me?"

Mrs. McKennedy nodded. "We have a little problem," she said as Tony walked past.

*　　*　　*

Tony passed by Arisa and the teacher, unconcerned with their conversation. He'd already put his luggage on the bus and was on his way back inside to assist his girlfriend.

"I'll help you with those, Reese." Tony took two of the suitcases from his girlfriend as he came up behind her in the hallway. He lightly kissed her cheek and she winked at him and began to walk down the hallway. Tony fell in step beside her.

"Are you ready for a wild and exciting week?" Tony raised his eyebrows and grinned as the pair walked out of the school.

"Always am." Reese smiled back.

The sun had begun to warm the autumn air. The leaves on the trees lining the parking lot already hinted at the colors they would be changing to soon. The day promised to be beautiful. A great way to start their trip.

*   *   *

As Mrs. McKennedy finished looking over her checklist, Arisa watched the students arrive. They gave their parents quick good-byes and made their way toward the bus, lugging with them their suitcases, sleeping bags and pillows all while talking excitedly with their friends. Arisa waved to some of her friends as they called out to her, smiling at their enthusiasm. Tony and Reese walked over to join her, smiling greetings at the younger kids.

"Looks like it's gonna be a beautiful day." Tony stuck his hands in his pockets after a quick glance at the pair of teachers standing behind Mrs. McKennedy.

After only a few minutes, twenty kids stood by the rented bus, waiting for instruction. Arisa glanced over at the teachers as Mrs. McKennedy raised her voice above the noise and shouted for everyone to be quiet. She paused as the students hushed and then she continued, motioning the student counselors to join her. "These are your counselors."

Arisa, Tony, and Reese walked over to where Mrs. McKennedy and two other teachers stood. Will followed them, leaving Candece and Ryan with the rest of the campers.

"We were supposed to have four teachers accompanying you. However, Mrs. Hernandaz phoned me late last night and informed me that she broke her leg yesterday and would be unable to go." This news was greeted by a groan from the campers. Mrs. Hernandaz was a favorite among the junior high. "This morning, I received a phone call from one of Mr. Edwards's children. They took him to the hospital last night and he has appendicitis. Neither teacher is in serious condition. They should be back in school soon. Mr. Brendan and Mrs. McNeil will be accompanying you but that leaves us short two adult counselors. I called the camp director and he assured me that two more adults would be assigned to you when you reach Camp Ventner. Your student counselors are Tony Vumeccelli, Reese Burnett, Will Johnson and Arisa McDonald. You are expected to obey them as you would one of your teachers." Mrs. McKennedy gave several students a stern look before continuing. "Better than you do to some teachers. If there are any problems on the trip, you will be dealt with severely upon your return."

*   *   *

Will Johnson smiled shyly as all eyes turned to look at the student counselors when their names were announced. Everyone already knew the gym teacher, David Brendan, and the fourth grade teacher, Jennifer McNeil. Arisa, Tony and Reese were all popular. Will was the only unknown. Will felt Tony sizing him up as he returned an appraising gaze. Reese smiled politely at Will for a second before returning her attention to Mrs. McKennedy. Sensing the young man's unease, Arisa stepped back to stand next to Will. As everyone turned back to Mrs. McKennedy, Arisa whispered to Will, "Relax. We're going to have fun." She smiled warmly.

Will returned the smile. Maybe this trip wouldn't be so bad after all.

"When you get to the airport, follow Mr. Brendan to the plane. Don't go wandering off. We don't want anyone getting lost. And that's about it. I'll see you on Thursday. Have fun!" Mrs. McKennedy turned and, with her back to the students, spoke to the student counselors, "have a good time. I'll see you when you get back."

"Mrs. McKennedy, could you take a picture of us before we

leave?" Twila handed a camera to the teacher. "Everyone, come here."

Will hung back, but Twila motioned him over. Several students joined the counselors and they all crowded together in front of the bus. "Ready? Smile." Mrs. McKennedy snapped the picture.

"Okay, let's load up." Mr. Brendan prompted. The kids moved towards the open doors, once more chattering away. Will followed Ryan and Candece onto the bus.

*   *   *

Mrs. McKennedy stood outside and watched as the kids got situated inside the bus. She waved at the students before walking back to the building. As she reached the doors, an uneasy feeling came over her. She stopped and looked back. "God, You will watch over them, won't You?" She prayed as the bus pulled away. She watched until it disappeared around the corner of the building and then turned to enter the school. As she did so, she realized she still held Twila's camera. With a sigh, she slipped it into the pocket of her jacket and shook her head to clear it.

*   *   *

Back on the bus, Arisa found herself seated next to a blond-haired boy she recognized from the previous year's junior high basketball team. She smiled at him before turning around to see where the other counselors were sitting. She spotted Tony and Reese at the back of the bus, his arm around her shoulders and her head resting against him. Mrs. McNeil was sitting directly behind the driver with her son, Jake, who didn't look too happy with the arrangement. Mr. Brendan was across the aisle and a few rows back from Arisa. Will sat closer to the front with his sister; his brother sat behind them with Twila.

Everyone cheered as the bus pulled out of the parking lot.

"Arisa!" Twila called to her sister before they had reached the highway.

"What's wrong?" Arisa made her way up the aisle, gripping the seat backs to keep her balance.

"I forgot to get my camera back from Mrs. McKennedy."

"Don't worry." Arisa patted her sister's shoulder. "I'll loan you my camera, okay? We can get double prints."

"Okay." Twila nodded, still disappointed.

"You can use mine too." Ryan offered shyly.

Twila smiled as Arisa made her way back to her seat. She

heard her sister thank the young man and begin a conversation about an idea she had involving still frames and digital film.

A few minutes later, some of the students began to sing church camp songs. When they started a familiar one, even the teachers joined in. About twenty minutes later, the bus reached the airport. Mr. Brendan was the first to his feet. Everyone remained sitting until he finished giving instructions and then began to move. Eager to get started, the students willingly complied and took only a few minutes to follow through.

Once they were sure everyone was off the bus, Mr. Brendan and Mrs. McNeil lead the students across the airport parking lot towards the small rental plane. Arisa fell into step next to Will who was helping Candece with her suitcase. Tony and Reese walked together at the back of the group, making sure none of the students were straggling behind. It didn't take long to reach their destination.

*   *   *

Tony grabbed fourteen year-old José Hendricks and the two of them began to load the kids' bags onto the plane. Out of the corner of his eye, Tony noticed a tall, thin man standing in front of the plane. His wild white hair stood on end, but it was his outlandish outfit that drew Tony's attention. With a smile, Tony noticed the man checking the engine of the plane before takeoff. Thanks to people like his parents, the school was usually over-concerned with their students' safety. Often, the administration went out of their way to make sure everything was in order, not wanting to risk a lawsuit.

"Hey, Reese." Tony called out melodramatically, "do you think you brought enough suitcases?"

"If you keep talking like that, don't expect any kisses from me. You're always so mean to me." Reese retorted, faking a pout. Tony grinned at her and readied a retaliatory reply but José interrupted before Tony could speak.

"Tony," José cut into the conversation. "That's the last of them."

"Okay, let's head back." He motioned for José to follow. They walked back to the group and Tony went over to Reese and Arisa while José returned to his girlfriend. "When we get on the plane, I think Mr. Brendan and Mrs. McNeil should take a role call, just in case some kids decided to wander away while we were loading up. I don't think we can trust these junior high kids very much."

"I don't either." Arisa agreed, grinning at Tony. "I remember what you were like in junior high, Tony. If these kids are that bad, we'll have our hands full."

"I wasn't bad." Tony protested. "I was – energetic." He grinned.

The four student counselors laughed as they joined the teachers. Mrs. McNeil quickly explained to them the new group assignments Mrs. McKennedy had come up with after the two other teachers called her. Originally, the students had been divided into four groups with one teacher and one student counselor for each group, but since Mrs. Hernandez's unfortunate accident and Mr. Edwards' emergency surgery, things had been reworked into two groups. Mr. Brendan explained that he would be in charge of the larger of the two groups, with Tony and Reese as the student counselors. They would split the kids between them and report to Mr. Brendan with any problems. Tony and Reese nodded in agreement as Mr. Brendan continued. Mrs. McNeil would be in charge of the smaller group, with Will and Arisa as the student counselors. This group was made up of the most hyperactive and mischievous students who would need more monitoring. At Arisa's request, Mrs. McKennedy had also included Twila, Candece and Ryan in their siblings' group. When the students finished getting onto the plane, Mr. Brendan explained the situation and handed Tony the list of students. Tony thanked the teacher and began to read off the names of his group while Mr. Brendan went to speak to the pilot.

"Mark Long and Jake McNeil."

Two young men sitting together raised their hands. Mark was a small, dark-skinned seventh grader; Jake was a year older and only slightly larger. Both were quiet and paid little attention to their surroundings, seeming to be more interested in their hand-held electronic games. Mark's skills in math and Jake's talent with computers had gained them admittance into the camp. Jake's presence was the only reason Mrs. McNeil had agreed to chaperone the trip; she hated any type of camping. He'd begged not to be put in her group and she'd reluctantly agreed.

"Amanda Whit and Joseph Black."

A couple sitting together raised their hands. The young woman's blond hair was pulled back tightly in a bun, giving her a mature look her actions denied. Though she was adept in science, she was far from the most socially skilled student at WCS. The young man next to her grinned and pushed his glasses up on his nose, running his other hand through his blond hair. They immediately turned their attention back to whatever they had been discussing, most likely science or computers, Joseph's specialty. Or perhaps debating the finer points of their lasting LARP adventure as characters from their favorite TV show.

Tony continued the role call. "Tammy and Randy Smith."

An athletic-looking girl with dark brown hair waved one hand in the air. Tammy was WCS's only professionally trained gymnast, and, therefore, captain of the cheerleading squad. She hoped to qualify for the next Olympics and used cheerleading as extra practice. Rumor had it that she had a strong shot at getting there.

Sitting next to Twila, in front of Tammy, was Tammy's older brother Randy, a talented musician who regularly lead praise and worship for WCS chapels. He glanced up at Tony and raised his hand in acknowledgment. His blue eyes sparkled. Even though he was just fourteen, Randy was almost as tall as Tony and had an amazing jump shot, which automatically gave him a spot on the varsity basketball squad.

Tony handed the list to Reese and pointed to the next set of names on the list. These students would be Reese's responsibility.

"Reba, Becky, and Melanie Jones."

Three similar-looking girls stopped talking only long enough to indicate their presence by a simultaneously loud and bubbly, "present!" Fourteen year-old Becky dramatically flipped her long dark hair over her shoulder as her younger sisters rolled their brown eyes at her attempts to flirt with Randy. All three Jones girls had been chosen for the trip for their many drama awards – they'd won first place in the ACSI (American Christian Schools Incorporated) Fine Arts Competition's drama category for the past two years. And all three were known among their peers for being totally boy crazy. '

"Tia and Renae Morgan."

Two dark-skinned girls raised their hands slowly. Tia was the younger of the two by a year. She handed the list to Arisa as the pilot and Mr. Brendan entered the plane. The pilot stood at the cockpit door, arms crossed over his thin chest.

"Nat Lewis."

A friendly looking fourteen year-old with dark brown curls smiled at Arisa who acknowledged her young friend by returning the smile. The two girls played volleyball, soccer and basketball together at WCS and had become friends through the tough summer practices as they juggled playing volleyball and soccer at the same time. Nat's singing abilities had earned her the ACSI Fine Arts Competition's first prize for two years and second prize her first year. Talent in singing was one of the things Nat and Arisa didn't have in common.

"José Hendricks."

The dark-haired young man next to Nat raised a hand. He, too, smiled at Arisa who smiled back. He also played soccer and had helped the girls learn new plays when they had to miss a practice. He was a good kid; sometimes he just needed something to help him burn off his extra energy – which was why he also played basketball and golf for WCS and played on a summer baseball team. His golf skills had given him a place at Camp Ventner.

"I know Twila's here." Arisa nodded at her younger sister and smiling. Twila returned the grin and turned back to reading her book.

"Luke White." Arisa called out the young man's name, looking around the bus. She knew this particular eighth grader would be one of the students needing a little more than minimal supervision. He was consistently getting into trouble though his intentions were usually innocent enough. His interest in computers and animation seemed to be the only thing able to keep him occupied for long periods of time; all the time he'd spent on his computer was now paying off. He'd never hidden his ambitions of becoming a computer animator for Hollywood and Camp Ventner seemed like a good place to get some training.

The boy who had been sitting next to Arisa on the bus shouted. "Back here!" His dark eyes sparkled as he took something out of his book bag. He aimed the rubber band at Arisa, but Mr. Brendan's headshake made him reconsider.

Arisa continued down the list. "Kris Roberts." A small boy with brown hair and glasses raised his hand as he laughed at his seatmate and best friend. He punched Luke's shoulder and Luke opened his mouth to complain. A sharp look from Arisa silenced them both.

"Tommy Martin."

Tommy sat with his girlfriend Tammy Smith, his pale green eyes and fiery hair sharply contrasted with the young woman's dark hair and eyes. Arisa checked her list and noted that Tommy had been marked as being hyperactive. She'd thought as much when she'd watched him at track meets over the past two years. He was already one of the top athletes in the area. Even after running, he never seemed tired. He promised to be quite a handful.

"Candece and Ryan Johnson." Thirteen year-old Candece sat in a window seat next to Will. Her light blue eyes lit up as she smiled.

Arisa looked behind Will to where his youngest brother, Ryan sat alone. He nodded at Arisa and pushed his glasses up his nose before returning his attention to *The Last Summer*.

Arisa handed the list back to Mr. Brendan who then informed the pilot that they were ready to leave. The pilot glared at the students from his different-colored eyes – one green, one brown.

"Finally." He muttered under his breath, turning toward the cockpit's entrance. His shock of white hair brushed the top of the doorway as he stepped inside.

"Hey, we had to be sure everyone was on the plane." Arisa muttered to herself as she sat next to Ryan, giving him a warm smile. The younger boy smiled back, his dark eyes warm. He held Arisa's gaze for only a few seconds before turning back to his book. He was already a quarter of the way into it; Arisa thought she'd seen him open to the first page when the bus was leaving the school.

Arisa retrieved her Bible from her book bag and opened it to her favorite passage. She began to read the thirty-seventh Psalm as the plane prepared for takeoff. She breathed a prayer as she struggled to calm her nerves. She'd never flown before and wasn't feeling too comfortable in the small plane. The pilot's appearance and sour attitude hadn't helped. "Lord God help me."

*   *   *

There were no further comments from George Reeves as he climbed into the cockpit. He glanced back at the kids, looking over them from their expensive shoes to their designer clothes and numerous electric toys. A smile spread across his face as he double-checked the small compartment behind his seat. Had any of the counselors or kids seen that smile, they might have thought twice about trusting him to fly their plane. He then slid into the pilot's seat and started the engine.

At last, nineteen seventh through ninth graders, four upperclassmen and two teachers set off for a camping trip that would change their lives.

*   *   *

After a little over an hour of flying, the more lively students began to get restless. The noise level grew and a few students unbuckled their belts and began to move around the cabin. A few others decided to stay seated but annoy their nearby classmates. Kris took Luke's rubber band and fired it at Tammy.

"Twila, tell your sister that Kris threw something at me!"

Tammy wailed melodramatically, putting a hand to the back of her head.

"Kris, cut it out." Arisa set her Bible aside with a frustrated sigh. She looked around the plane for the other counselors. Mr. Brendan, susceptible to air sickness, had told the counselors he planned to take sleeping pills before takeoff; he was now snoring away in his seat. Mrs. McNeil looked annoyed, but seemed unsure of herself around the older students. Arisa had often heard her comment that she wasn't fond of children over the age of ten. Will was also looking around and he caught Arisa's gaze. He started to stand but Arisa shook her head and he sat back down. She continued looking for Tony and Reese. Finally, she spotted them sitting alone in the back of the plane. They weren't paying much attention to anyone but each other.

Arisa motioned to Mrs. McNeil who stood up and walked back to where Tony and Reese sat, their arms entwined and their lips together, barely pausing to come up for air. The teacher stood silently in the aisle for a second before clearing her throat and speaking loud enough to attract everyone's attention. "I really hate to bother you two, but if I could have a moment of your time."

Tony and Reese pulled apart, faces flushed. Reese's face turned red with embarrassment as Tony began wiping her bright red lipstick from his mouth.

"What's wrong?" Tony tried to act nonchalant.

"First of all, there's the no PDA rule, which doesn't just apply when you're on school grounds." Mrs. McNeil replied, a scowl on her face. "What type of example do you think you're setting for these kids? All physical issues aside, you're showing them that you have no respect for the rules. Secondly, your job here is to watch these students, not have a date with your girlfriend. With Mr. Brendan sleeping through the flight, I expected a little more help from you two."

Tony looked around, abashed by the reprimand. All activity had come to a halt at some point during Mrs. McNeil's lecture and now all eyes were on the couple. A ripple of laughter moved around the group as several students could hold back their amusement no longer.

Arisa smiled and tried to keep from joining in as she looked at her friend's face, unable to meet his eyes for fear of losing control. Her anger melted as she began to chuckle, hand over her mouth to stifle her laughter. Only Mrs. McNeil failed to see the humor in the situation and continued to glare at Tony, arms crossed over her chest.

"What is it?" Tony asked, annoyed that the students were laughing at him for no reason he could see. He looked around, trying to see the cause of everyone's laughter. The harder he looked and the more frustrated he became, the harder the kids laughed. Even Reese began to giggle as a bright blush of realization crept up her cheeks.

While Arisa pulled a tissue from her pocket, Reese dug into her purse. She handed Tony a mirror and he flushed as he saw the red lipstick smudges. He took Arisa's pro-offered tissue and began scrubbing his lips, scowling angrily at no one in particular. The harder he scrubbed the harder the kids laughed. After a minute or so, he stood and stalked to the back of the plane, refusing to look at anyone.

Arisa's laughter was cut short as she was suddenly thrown off balance. The windows rattled and the plane began to shake. The kids struggled to get back in their seats and their belts fastened as Arisa and Mrs. McNeil tried to keep them calm. Arisa gave them shaky smiles as she made her way up the aisle. She ignored the fear in her own gut as she repeated that it was only a little turbulence, managing to keep her voice steady. As Tony came out of the bathroom, Arisa gave him a worried glance as he moved to where his girlfriend stood. Tony looked from Arisa to Reese, their concern mirrored on his face.

Mrs. McNeil carefully made her way up the aisle and stood next to Becky, who was clutching the armrests of her seat so tightly her knuckles were white. Arisa looked back and saw Tony and Reese move up to stand next to a worried Jake and Amanda. Will looked over at them from where he now sat behind his siblings. The four student counselors exchanged glances, anxiety written in all of their eyes. Tony put his arm around Reese, pulling her close in an effort to comfort her. Arisa watched him whisper something in his girlfriend's ear and she smiled weakly.

Leaving the pair to reassure each other, Arisa turned her attention to Will. He glanced at her and offered a wan smile as he continued to talk with his brother and sister. They were calm and Will continued to talk with them softly, leaning forward, his voice low enough that Arisa couldn't make out the words.

As the plane continued its downward descent, Mark looked out his window and saw the dark ocean water drawing closer. His voice came out barely above a whisper. "We're going to crash."

Amanda, near enough to hear Mark, let out a bloodcurdling scream. Panic broke out. The counselors struggled to keep the students calm, shouting over the screams to no avail. Mrs. McNeil motioned for Arisa to talk to the pilot while she attempted to wake Mr. Brendan from his medicinal slumber.

Arisa made her way to the cockpit and peered in the tiny window. Her stomach lurched and she grabbed the wall to keep herself steady. She forced herself to turn and walk calmly down the aisle again, praying her face wouldn't betray her. She immediately went to Mrs. McNeil and told her what she'd seen. The teacher's face went white and her mouth opened into a wide O. Her hands flew to her face and she attempted to speak, but nothing came out. She sat heavily in the seat next to Mr. Brendan as Arisa walked past Candece and Ryan. She leaned down next to Will and whispered to him what she'd told Mrs. McNeil. His face went pale and he immediately instructed Candece and Ryan to stay put and cover their heads. Arisa reached for his hand and squeezed it. Will returned the pressure, trying to convey some strength to the young woman before she turned and continued down the aisle. Will stood and repeated his instructions to the other students.

Arisa reached Reese next. She stood next to a still hysterical Amanda, trying to soothe the young woman. Tony had moved to calm Mark. "Stay calm." Arisa hissed into Reese's ear, trying to keep her own voice from shaking. "There's no one in the cockpit. Walk over to Tony and tell him. We can't let the kids know, but we need to get their seat belts on and get them to cover their heads. The door's locked and we're going down.

We will crash."

Reese's face went white.

"I'll stay with Amanda." Arisa smiled down at the student. Amanda grabbed Arisa's hand in a grip so tight it was painful.

Reese began to walk back to Tony.

The impact threw everyone forward. Some of the kids crashed into the seats in front of them, blacking out from the blow. Others were thrown into the aisles, their belts torn away from the fabric of the seats. Junk flew from compartments as doors opened.

Arisa's ears filled with the sounds of metal crunching against metal and the whining sound of scraping against water and rock. She felt herself flying through the air and closed her eyes. She was only vaguely aware of pain in her body as she hit one of the cabin walls and slid to the floor. The only thing she knew for sure was that the people around her were screaming.

Chapter Two

The screaming stopped.

Nothing moved.

No one breathed.

Arisa blinked and shook her head to clear it, wincing at the pain that shot through her temples. She felt something warm and sticky running down the right side of her face and lifted a hand, wiping her cheek. Her fingers came away smeared a brilliant red. A jagged cut across her cheek oozed blood, mixing with the dust covering her face. It throbbed but Arisa ignored the pain as the thought of her sister came first into her mind; immediately following were thoughts of her friends and her other traveling companions.

Arisa got to her feet, biting her lip to hold back the moan of pain as every muscle in her body protested the movement. She looked around at the destruction.

The collision had torn a gaping hole across the front of the plane, ripping off the cockpit and a large chunk of the roof. Arisa could hear water lapping up against the metal and knew if she looked outside, she'd see the ocean. Just how much time they had before the water started to come inside, she didn't know. She pushed the thought from her mind as she checked herself for injuries.

While her whole body ached, her cheek and left hand seemed to be her only actual injuries. A shard of metal had embedded itself deep into the back of her hand, just above her wrist. She gritted her teeth, pulled the metal splinter out and then changed her focus once more, looking around for survivors. A sudden movement near the back of the plane caught her eye. As she turned towards the motion, others began to stir, breaking the eerie silence with groans of pain.

Arisa started to move toward the figure when her foot hit against something soft and yielding. She looked down. An arm protruded from the rubble, motionless and covered with blood. Its wrist hung at an awkward angle. A sickly white bone stuck out of a section of ripped skin in the forearm. Arisa dropped to her knees and managed to push the plane seat off the two students it had crushed.

"Dear, God, no." She breathed, feeling sick. She reached out and tentatively touched Amanda's neck, feeling for a pulse she knew wouldn't be present. She then turned to Joseph and repeated the pointless gesture. She swallowed hard, fighting the burning sensation in the pit of her stomach and the urge to panic.

"Twila! Mrs. McNeil! Tony! Will! Reese!" She called, her voice choked as she fought back her nausea. Only now did she allow herself to recognize the fear at the back of her mind that her sister or one of her friends would be among the dead.

"Arisa." A soft voice made Arisa look up. José made his way toward her. His eyes were wide and his expression dazed as he walked across the rubble, not really seeing where he was going.

"Stop! Listen to me José. I need you to go find Mrs. McNeil or Mr. Brendan while I look for Twila. Can you do that?" Arisa held up a hand and José stopped. She knew she had to protect the survivors from seeing their dead classmates. José nodded slightly and turned away. Arisa fought back another wave of nausea, refusing to allow herself to throw up. She took a deep breath and swallowed hard, praying she wouldn't pass out. She had to find Twila and didn't have time to lose the little bit of breakfast she'd eaten.

Moans began to fill the once quiet air as others regained consciousness. All felt their injured and throbbing heads, some in worse shape than others.

Groaning, Reese propped herself up against the wall of the plane and tried to stand, wincing as she straightened. Her legs wobbled and almost didn't hold her. Bruises had already formed across both of her forearms from hitting the seats. Some minor scratches across her face and arms were bleeding, but nothing felt serious. She stretched out her arm and sucked in a sharp breath as a stab of pain shot up her wrist. She started to cry.

Arisa saw her friend crying and moved toward the young woman. She wiped again at the blood on her cheek as she made her way to Reese. Suddenly, something grabbed her ankle. Arisa stopped and looked down. It was a hand, covered in blood, the knuckles white from the grip it had on her ankle. Arisa grabbed the seat, ignoring the jagged edges cutting into her palms, and lifted it off of Will. He had twisted onto his side and avoided being crushed by the seat, but his arms had been pinned.

"Thank you." He gasped. His left arm was bleeding from shoulder to below his elbow, almost to his wrist. A broken piece of the seat had cut him as it fell; if he hadn't rolled, the metal would have cut into his chest and stomach with what would have been fatal wounds. A few smaller cuts crossed his legs, staining his torn jean shorts with blood. Will was unconcerned with his own injuries, thinking only of his brother and sister. "Ryan and Candece. Where are they?" He held his right hand over the cut on his arm, trying to stop the bleeding as he sat up.

"I don't know, but I'm sure they're okay." Arisa looked at

Will's arm, untucked her shirt, and ripped the clean section off the bottom of it. She wrapped the cloth around the worst part of the cut and tied it tightly, giving him an apologetic look when he winced with pain. She tried to give Will a reassuring smile, but he could read the fear in her eyes as she stood up. He reached out with his good arm and grabbed her hand, giving it a quick squeeze of reassurance. Arisa returned the gesture, released his hand and then walked back towards Reese, she saw Will stand and move forward to where Candece and Ryan had been sitting.

Arisa spoke to Reese as soon as she was close enough for the older girl to hear her. "You okay?"

"Where's Tony?" Reese's voice was shrill. More dirt than blood covered Reese's face and Arisa breathed a sigh of relief that her friend appeared to be okay. The situation was bad enough. Arisa prayed that Tony was also uninjured. Losing him would be unbearable; not only was he a close friend but Arisa wasn't sure Reese could handle losing Tony.

"I'm right here, Reese and I'm okay," a voice came from the back of the plane. Tony quickly came towards the girls, stepping around debris. "Becky is..." Tony couldn't say the word. Reese looked puzzled but Arisa nodded and put a hand on Reese's arm. She looked from Arisa's grim face to Tony's white one and gasped, understanding showing in her horrified expression. Tony looked like he wanted to throw up and Arisa didn't blame him. He stepped past Arisa and wrapped his arms around Reese. She buried her face in Tony's chest, soft cries turning into sobs.

"There wasn't anything I could do." His voice cracked. He cleared his throat. When he continued, his voice was controlled, but he struggled to keep it that way. "Reba and Melanie are okay. Melanie has a cut on her leg and her wrist is probably broken, but there aren't any bones sticking out. I think Reba cracked some of her fingers when she tried to shield her face from the seat in front of her. I should splint them so they don't get worse." As he was talking, Reese looked up at him, the question written in her eyes. "Just a few scrapes and bruises, honey. Nothing major."

Arisa felt her heart go out to Tony. She knew he'd always wanted to be a doctor. He hated seeing anyone in pain; having a student under his care die where there was nothing he could have done to prevent it – or help them – hit close to his heart.

"Where're Mrs. McNeil and Mr. Brendan?" Arisa asked. As the words left her mouth, a blood-chilling scream echoed through the plane, raising cries of fright from already terrified students. Arisa immediately turned. It was Twila. She hurried back to where Twila was sitting. Mark lay next to her. Arisa turned away and fought to control her stomach as Twila shakily got to her feet.

"Arisa! He's d-dead! He's dead!" Twila buried her face in Arisa's shoulder. Arisa held her sister close, thanking God the girl was okay. Twila kept talking, unable to stop herself. "I thought we were all dead. I thought I'd be dead, and you'd be dead and everyone would be dead."

"Shh. It's all right. We're going to be fine." Arisa soothed her sobbing sister. "We're okay. We'll be okay. We're all going to be okay." Arisa murmured the words she wasn't sure she herself believed.

"Jake's over there." José came up behind Twila and Arisa, face chalk-white. He motioned to the far corner of the plane. "He's dead, too." A large bruise under his eye promised a black eye and a scratch down his cheek oozed blood, but they appeared to be the extent of his injuries. Nat stood behind him in shocked silence, seemingly uninjured. She reached out to José. The young man took his girlfriend's hand and pulled her to him, keeping his arm around her as they followed Arisa and Twila back to Reese and Tony.

"What about Mrs. McNeil and Mr. Brendan?" Arisa asked. She breathed a sigh of relief when she saw Will with Candece and Ryan. Both were pale and shaking, but didn't seem badly hurt.

"I found them." Will spoke in a hoarse voice. "Mrs. McNeil," he stopped and shook his head. "I don't know about Mr. Brendan. He's hurt... bad."

"Tony, you go. See what you can do." Arisa said. Tony whispered something softly in Reese's ear and released her. Reese clung to him, forcing Tony to disentangle himself and pull away. With a reassuring look to his girlfriend, he headed in the direction Will pointed.

Arisa gathered the rest of the survivors together at the front of the plane while Will disappeared in the direction of the cockpit. By the time everyone had huddled together, Will returned and whispered his news in Arisa's ear. She nodded once, mouth tight, but didn't say anything yet. The other students were looking to her to set an example. Completely numbed by what had happened, the kids clung to each other, making little noise as they cried. They huddled together, unsure what to do next.

"C-can everyone walk?" Arisa's voice shook and she fought to steady it. Several nods and mumbled words answered her question.

"My shoulder hurts." Renae cried, her voice becoming shrill

as she tried to move her arm. She screamed, piercing the air.

"Don't move, Renae. It'll be okay." Arisa glanced over at Tony as he joined the group. Following Arisa's gaze, he walked over to Renae and felt her injured shoulder. She screamed again and pulled away. Tony spoke to her softly, shooting a look to Arisa and confirming what she'd suspected. Renae's shoulder was dislocated.

Tony led Renae off to one side and motioned for Will to help him. He kept his voice low and even as he talked Renae through what he was going to do. Tony picked up a shirt from the floor of the plane.

"This is going to hurt, but it'll keep your shoulder from moving until we get somewhere a doctor can look at it." Tony took Renae's wrist in hand, jarring her arm. The girl's eyes rolled back as she passed out. Will caught her and held her as Tony quickly immobilized her arm. The pair then carried the girl to her sister and laid her on the floor. Twila moved to sit by the unconscious girl's side.

"Tony," Arisa pulled him aside once he'd finished with Renae.

"Mrs. McNeil's dead." Tony kept his voice low so the students wouldn't hear him. "Mr. Brendan's alive, but unconscious. He got pretty banged up. I don't know how badly he's hurt or if he'll make it. I don't know what to do."

Arisa nodded and raised her voice to get everyone's attention. "We're not sinking, so we can assume we're okay for now. Now, Will's already checked the plane's radio and it's not working, so we need to know if anyone has a cell phone."

Kids exchanged dazed looks before Randy spoke up. "We were told not to bring them."

Arisa raised an eyebrow. "Yeah, and you're not supposed to have them in school either." She scanned the group. "Who has one?"

After a moment, Reba and Melanie raised their hands. "There's no signal though." Melanie said, handing over her phone.

"That would make things too easy, wouldn't it." Arisa muttered as she confirmed what Melanie had said. She glanced in Tony's direction. "At least we have them."

Tony nodded in agreement and added. "We need you to look for anything that might be useful. Bandages, water, anything you think might be helpful."

"Bring the bags over to the door." Will added. As the students moved to do as they'd been asked, Will told Arisa he'd try to get a better assessment of their situation.

Ten minutes later, most of the students gathered again at the front of the plane, bringing with them whatever they could find. Tony and Arisa tore some of the clothes into strips that they then combined with whatever they could find to immobilize the more serious injuries. Ryan had a few broken toes but he was able to walk. Candece had twisted her ankle, but insisted she was okay. Reese whimpered with pain when Tony touched her wrist, but after he examined and found it to be only a sprain, she allowed Tony to wrap it and then, without further complaints, started to help Arisa and Tony. The trio worked quickly. They finished just as Will returned with information and Luke and Kris appeared with a package.

"What is that?" Reese eyed the boys' burden.

"A raft." Luke was serious.

"And what are we supposed to do with that?" Reese asked sharply.

"Give us a minute guys." Arisa spoke to the students while motioning for her friends to come away from the group. "Reese, calm down. These two..."

"Calm down?" Reese's voice started to rise but dropped down when Tony grabbed her arm. "How can you tell me to calm down after what just happened?"

"Because if you're not calm, the kids aren't going to be calm." Arisa spoke through clenched teeth. "I'm not enjoying this anymore than you are, but since we don't have any adults here, it's our responsibility to take charge."

"She's right." Tony cut off the protest before Reese could form it. "We have to figure out what we're going to do."

"Randy gave me this." Arisa handed a folded piece of paper to Tony.

Tony unfolded the map and spread it out on the ground, bending down so he could study it more closely.

"What did you find?" Arisa turned to Will. He glanced at Luke and Will. Arisa took the raft from them. "Thanks guys. Why don't you join the rest of the kids?"

They nodded and went back to the group without argument. Once they were gone, Will quickly filled the others in on what he'd discovered.

"We need to get as many people as possible off of this plane." Arisa began reading the instructions on the side of the package.

"And where exactly are we going to put them?" Reese raised an eyebrow.

"There's island not too far from here. It's got a decent-sized resort. We should be able to get help there." Tony looked up from the map.

"There's no way that raft is going to hold all of us." Reese shook her head.

"You're right. It'll take ten." Arisa agreed.

"That's stupid!" Reese's voice rose again.

"Reese!" Tony's voice was harsh. "We can't all stay here and hope someone flying over rescues us."

"Come on, Tony, this isn't some movie. Someone'll be looking for us in a few hours, if they haven't spotted us already." Reese continued to argue but her voice had dropped back down. "We shouldn't split up."

"I agree." Will nodded. "It's a bad idea to break up the group."

"I think so too, but there isn't another option." Arisa looked down at Tony.

Tony sighed and stood up, refolding the map and putting it in his pocket. "We can't guarantee how long this plane will stay here. If there's a storm before help comes..." His voice trailed off for a moment.

"So we take our chances." Reese grabbed Tony's hand.

"I'm not gambling with the lives of all of these kids." Arisa crossed her arms over her chest. "If we use the raft, at least most of them get off."

"We have to send at least two counselors." Will spoke up and the other three turned their attention to him. "You'd have to take Mr. Brendan and he'll need someone looking after him. He's in the worst condition and needs medical help more than anyone else."

Tony nodded in agreement. "I think that's the best choice."

"Tony!" Reese's eyes welled up with tears. "We shouldn't leave the plane."

"We can't just sit and do nothing." Tony put his arm around Reese's shoulders and pulled her to him. He pressed his lips to her hair. "It'll be okay." He looked at Arisa. "Let's tell them."

"Okay, listen up!" Arisa called. All eyes turned towards her. "Luke and Kris found a raft made to hold ten people." A murmur ran through the group. There were eighteen survivors, far too many to attempt to cram into the raft.

Tony continued. "Two of us, Mr. Brendan, and as many of you as possible will get on the raft. The rest of you will stay here with the other two counselors. Will," the young man flushed with embarrassment, "went up front to see why the plane isn't sinking and he says we're stuck on a sandbar. According to a map Randy found and how far I'm guessing we traveled, there should be an island resort around here somewhere; that's where we're heading. Any questions?"

"Which of you are staying with me?" Will spoke softly, but all eyes turned to him. The flush on his face deepened. None of

the counselors had asked each other who was going to stay –
no one wanted to voice the question.

"I am." Arisa said.

Reese flashed Arisa a heartfelt smile as Tony glanced the
younger girl's way, worry mixed with his immense gratitude.
Both Reese and Tony looked relieved as they nodded in
agreement. Arisa and Will's lack of hesitation while they
struggled with indecision had made both uncomfortable, but
they didn't argue the decision.

Tony poised the next question. "We need volunteers to stay
with them. If no one volunteers, we'll have to draw names."

Silence blanketed the plane.

"I'll stay." Nat broke the silence. Her dark eyes were wide
with fright, but her face was determined.

"I guess I will, too." José said, reluctant to stay but even
more reluctant to leave without his girlfriend. He put his other
arm around Nat, hugging her close.

"Please, guys. Don't make us choose." Arisa pleaded with
the remaining kids, hating she had to ask but hating the
alternative more.

"I'll stay." Luke said finally.

"I'm staying." Twila spoke up, her face pale, voice firm.

"No!" Arisa spoke sharply. She shook her head.

"If you're staying, so am I." Twila locked eyes with Arisa. An unspoken word passed between the sisters.

Arisa took a deep breath and spoke again, a hint of defeat mingled with sisterly pride in her voice. "I guess I can't talk you out of it." She paused, then added, "but if I get grounded because I let you stay, I am *so* returning your birthday present." After another moment of sisterly silence, Arisa turned to the rest of the kids. "Anyone else?"

"If Luke's staying, then I am, too." Kris said. "Best friends need to stick together and look out for each other. Besides, I can't let him get all the glory for volunteering while I chickened out. It's a chance for a real adventure."

"Nice monologuing." Luke grinned.

"Thanks." Kris held up a hand and Luke slapped it.

"I'll stay," Tommy said.

"Thank you." Arisa looked at each of the students who had volunteered. They met her steady gaze with frightened, but determined ones' of their own. They understood what they were doing.

Tony spoke up. "We should go. Will, can you and Randy get Mr. Brendan? He should be okay to move." The two young men nodded and left the group to retrieve the injured teacher.

"We're going to be okay." Arisa tried to reassure the kids around her with a voice that threatened to break. She squelched the panic rising in her throat and prayed for strength. She let out a breath as she felt the Holy Spirit wash over her with a flood of peace.

Tony led the way to the door of the small plane. Neither the ones going nor the ones staying spoke. No one knew what to say. There were no words – not even from the most talkative of them.

Arisa grabbed an armload of clothes from the floor and handed the bundle to Reese. "You might need more bandages."

Reese nodded.

Tony looked from Arisa to the students and then spoke. "Say your good-byes now." He managed to keep his voice as steady as possible. Arisa put a hand on her friend's shoulder and gave it a squeeze. He turned to look at her. "What about..." His voice trailed off, eyes darting off to one side. He didn't say anything else, but Arisa knew what he wanted to ask.

"I'll take care of them later." Arisa's face paled but she managed to keep her voice steady.

"Are you sure?" Tony looked concerned. Arisa took a deep breath and nodded, praying she'd have the strength to follow through.

"Thank you." Reese gave Arisa a wobbly smile.

The group parted, making room for Will and Randy. Mr. Brendan was over six feet tall and weighed at least two hundred pounds. By the time Will and Randy reached the door, they were panting with exertion. Students watched with wide eyes, hands clamped over their mouths to contain exclamations of shock and horror. The unconscious teacher was pale. Tony had bandaged the right side of Mr. Brendan's head and the white material stood out in sharp contrast to the dirt and blood-covered skin.

"Let's get going." Tony said. The students leaving stepped forward.

Arisa stood at the back of the group of remaining kids, her arm around her sister's shoulders. Will came and stood beside her. He smiled and put a hand on her shoulder. Arisa covered his hand with hers, afraid that if she tried to smile, her composure would crack.

"We'll bring back some pizza." Tony said as he and Randy tugged on the plane door.

Most of the kids smiled at Tony's comment but no one laughed.

The door came open easier than Arisa had expected. Bright afternoon sunlight streamed into the plane through the doorway. Arisa held a hand up to shield her face as Tony carefully lowered himself out of the plane and into the cold ocean water covering the several feet of sandbar that stuck out from under the plane.

"Here, you can use these to paddle." Luke leaned out of the doorway and handed Tony two long pieces of metal that looked like they had been part of a seat. Luke returned to his spot in front of Arisa.

Arisa reached out and took Twila's hand. The younger girl gave her sister a grateful look, needing the comfort. Will put a hand on Arisa's back, trying to convey his support. She looked back at him, the edges of her mouth curving slightly in the beginnings of a smile.

As Arisa stood and watched, the others climbed down into the raft. After everyone else was in, Tony, Randy and Will worked together to lower Mr. Brendan into the raft. The students on the plane waved as Tony climbed in next to Reese and pushed off.

After a few moments, she and Will were alone with the remaining six students. They all watched as the raft faded in the distance. As it disappeared, Will moved forward and shut the plane door, shutting out what light had still been coming in. The only light now came from the hole in the front of the plane.

Arisa took a deep breath and tried to sound cheerful. "So, what do you want to do while we wait?"

Her question was met by silence and stares. Finally, Nat suggested sorting through the debris. They could find any undamaged personal items to take with them when the rescue came.

"Good idea." Arisa moved over to where several suitcases had broken open. She turned to the kids and said, "come on." Her voice held a note of desperation. They all knew that nothing really needed to be done, but they also knew there was no other way to get their minds off of their current situation.

One by one, the students left their places by the door and joined the rest of their group, sitting down in a lopsided circle. Will and Arisa stood outside the group for several minutes, watching as the kids began sifting through the mishmash of junk. As the minutes ticked by, the kids began to talk and the mood lightened. The oppressive air that had crowded around them eased and they all began to breathe easier. Will leaned down and whispered to Arisa. "I think now that they're distracted, the... bodies... should be taken care of."

"You're right. I'll do it now." Arisa started to move.

"No." Will protested. "I don't think you should... I'll take care of it. You just make sure the kids don't see what I'm doing."

"Are you sure?" Arisa turned to look at Will.

Will nodded. "A friend of mine back in Fort Prince worked at a funeral home. I used to help out some on weekends."

"Um, I don't really know how to respond to that." Arisa admitted.

"We needed the extra money and they had a hard time finding people willing to work around... you know." Will shrugged.

After a moment, Arisa gave Will a half-smile and squeezed his hand. "Thanks."

As Will moved away from the group, Arisa joined the others. She sat down between her sister and Nat, smiling at both of the girls as she tucked her legs under her. She didn't join in the conversation, but listened to the others as she watched Will out of the corner of her eye. Arisa breathed a prayer of thanks that the kids were filtering out everything outside their group; whether purposeful or not, she didn't know. She was just thankful they didn't acknowledge what Will was doing. After he'd finished, he joined them, sitting beside Arisa. He winced as he bumped his arm against her. Arisa looked down, noticing traces of blood already seeping through the dirt-covered bandage.

"You need that changed." Arisa spoke softly but her voice contained a reprimand.

"We've all had a lot on our mind." Will shrugged. "I'll get to it later."

"I'll do it." Arisa reached into a pile of clothes and took out a shirt. "Come here."

"Don't ruin one of your shirts." Will protested as he followed her off to one side. "It's no big deal."

"Hush." Arisa ripped the T-shirt into strips. This time, she made sure she did it correctly, the way Tony had shown her, pulling the edges of the cut together as she wrapped the arm. Will sucked in air as Arisa pulled the knot tight. He nodded his thanks, his face pale. They both turned back to the kids.

The afternoon crept into evening as the students waited for their friends to return, but inevitably, darkness stole over the plane and no rescue came. Gradually, the kids stretched out on the floor, huddling together for warmth. Will and Arisa watched as the kids fell asleep, their troubles forgotten as they slept. As another two hours passed, Will and Arisa sat in silence. Arisa finally lay down, feeling the exhaustion of the day taking over. Will lay behind her, watching until she slept. Only when he was certain everyone was asleep did he close his eyes and allow himself to sleep.

Chapter Three

"How long do you think we'll be out here?" Reese broke
the silence.

They'd been floating for hours, and now the sun was slowly
sinking down into the watery horizon. Mr. Brendan lay in the
middle of the raft. He hadn't woken yet, but the shallow rise
and fall of his chest assured the students that he was still alive.

"Maybe a couple more hours. Maybe another day." Tony
answered quietly. "Only God knows." He handed off his
makeshift paddle and stretched his cramped muscles.

"I sure wish He'd share it with us." Reese muttered under
her breath, tears welling up in her eyes.

Tony pulled his girlfriend close to him. The young man
swallowed hard against the lump rising in his throat as he
thought of his friends back on the plane. His trust that God
would get them safely off was quickly waning. He'd never had
his faith put to this kind of test and wasn't sure he would pass.

"The sun's going down." Tammy stated softly, a note of
fear creeping into her voice. "It'll be getting dark soon. Will
we go to sleep then?"

"That sounds like a good idea, Tammy." Tony tightened his
arm around Reese's shoulders as a cool ocean breeze blew
across the raft. He rubbed his hand down Reese's shoulder and

bare arm as she shivered from the chill in the air. She moved closer to Tony.

"Why don't we get out the sleeping bags and pull on an extra set of clothes. It's getting chilly and it's probably only going to get colder." Tony suggested. He breathed a prayer of thanks that Arisa had thought to send the extra clothes.

The kids followed his direction and pulled on various articles of clothing, using whatever looked as if they'd fit. After they finished, they began settling into the most comfortable positions they could find and pulling sleeping bags over them. Tony covered Mr. Brendan and the teacher still didn't stir. At a look from Tony, Randy pulled the paddles into the raft and leaned back against the side. Gradually, the kids fell into a deep, exhausted sleep that the most stressful situations often bring about. The last two people to go to sleep were Tony and Reese, arms wrapped around each other. Everyone on the raft was asleep before the final bit of sun disappeared.

*   *   *

A thin shaft of early morning sunlight shone in on Arisa's face, waking her from a restless slumber. She sat up, squinting into the bright light streaming in through the front of the plane. She shook her head to clear away the fogginess of sleep. She closed her eyes and took a deep breath. The air was stale. Even the opening at the front end of the plane didn't bring in enough fresh air to clear away the smell of death hanging in the air.

Arisa shuddered at the memories flooding back into her mind. She looked around, trying to orient herself. To her right were the items the students had sorted from the debris the night before. On one side of the pile were Luke, Kris, Nat, José, Twila, and Tommy, still sleeping. A few feet away from where she was lying was Will. Arisa felt her stomach churn as she remembered the bodies of the students whom Will had been forced to dispose of the previous night – bodies of kids she had known for years. As the plane warmed, she felt justified in her decision to dump the bodies. The day would probably be hot and they didn't know when their rescue would come. Her eyes welled up and she roughly brushed her hands across her cheeks. She winced and looked down, sighing as she saw blood on her hand from the reopened wound on her cheek. Arisa grabbed one of the cloth strips she'd torn to bandage Will's arm the night before and pressed it to her cheek, the fresh pain driving any remaining drowsiness from her mind.

The still slumbering students all appeared to be deep asleep despite the previous day's events. They were fortunate to be able to lose themselves in a few hours of uninterrupted, blissful sleep. When they woke, they would be forced to return to the reality of what had happened. Arisa allowed them to continue sleeping.

Arisa stood, moving as quietly as possible, and walked over to closest the window and peered out into the bright morning. The ocean was flat; not a thing could be seen across the wide expanse. The sky was clear. Barely a cloud across the blue and nothing marring the perfect canvas.

With a frustrated sigh, Arisa sat down and leaned her head back against the wall of the plane. She closed her eyes and began to pray silently, letting a warm wave of peace wash over her. Within moments, she was asleep.

Several hours passed before another person in the plane stirred. Luke was the first, followed by Twila and then Kris each woken by the others' movements. The three sat together for several minutes before becoming so uncomfortable with being the only ones awake in the plane that they decided it was time to get Arisa up.

"Arisa, wake up." Luke shook Arisa gently.

She opened her eyes slowly and stretched, yawning as she sat up and asked for the time.

"I don't know, probably about ten or eleven." Luke said, shrugging.

"How long have you been up?" Arisa looked around. The rest of the kids were still sleeping soundly on the floor of the plane. Will was just waking beside her. They smiled at each other, grateful for the company.

"Only for about ten minutes or so." Twila answered.

"I must have fallen asleep again. I was awake earlier." Arisa stood and stretched her arms above her head, her fingers stopping several inches short of touching the top of the cabin. She retrieved a brush from the floor, ran it through her hair and then braided the thick locks.

"How long do you think it will take for them to get back?" Twila asked, anxious eyes betraying her casual tone. She moved closer to Arisa who motioned for the younger girl to sit down in front of her. Twila did so and Arisa braided her sister's hair while they talked.

"I don't know." Arisa answered truthfully. She put her arm around Twila, trying to give her some comfort.

"What are we going to do for food?" Kris asked suddenly.

"There's still the airplane food. It may be nasty, but at least it's edible." Arisa motioned to the small cupboard near the back of the plane where the snacks had been kept. About thirty packages of nuts and fruit were scattered across the floor.

"Food?" A sleepy voice came from behind them. "Did someone say food?"

"I knew Tommy would wake up as soon as anyone mentioned food." Luke laughed. The young man leapt to his feet, and began pacing the length of the plane.

"We need to wake up the rest of the kids and get something to eat. We shouldn't sleep all day so we're ready when rescue comes." Arisa walked over to where the other students were sleeping. She bent down and gently shook Nat awake while Will and Luke woke the others. Within a few minutes, all of the students were awake and rummaging through the packages for anything that looked remotely edible.

"Arisa, fruit." Will grabbed a few packages of dried fruit and nuts. He tossed one of the packages to Arisa as he walked toward her.

"I'm not hungry. You can have it." Arisa smiled apologetically. She tossed the package back. Will nodded and sat down next to her. With a sigh, Arisa leaned her head back against the wall of the plane and silently prayed. "God, why us? Why us?"

* * *

Tony woke up slowly, the early morning sunlight shining in his face as it appeared over the horizon. He looked around; everyone else was still asleep. He sighed. At least the kids could forget their problems as they slept. Tony checked on Mr. Brendan again. He was still unconscious and Tony feared the teacher might have slipped into a coma. If they didn't reach land soon... Tony didn't even want to think about the consequences. He breathed an anxious prayer.

"Is it morning already?" Reese murmured. She turned to face Tony.

"Shh. It's early. You can go back to sleep." Tony whispered, not wanting to disturb the others. He smiled at his girlfriend and tenderly brushed a strand of dark hair back from her face.

"That's okay." Reese sat up and snuggled close to him.

Tony put his arm around her shoulders and pulled her to him. They both leaned back against the edge of the raft and watched the sunrise. Despite their circumstances, they found themselves entranced by the beauty of the morning. Both of them sat in silence as time moved on, unnoticed as each became lost in their own thoughts.

Two hours passed before anyone else on the raft woke.

Candece was the first. She yawned and stretched as she groggily blinked her eyes. She looked around before bringing her gaze to rest on Tony and Reese. "Any sign of land?" She asked.

"No." Tony answered after glancing around once more, praying he would see something. "It's still early. Go back to sleep again if you want to."

"No thank you." Candece looked down at Ryan who was still sleeping next to her and then back up at her counselor. "Reese?"

"Yes?" Reese managed a wan smile.

"Are you scared?" Candece's eyes were wide, making her look younger than she was.

"We're all scared sweetie." Reese reached out and squeezed Candece's hand. Reese's fingers were as cold as Candece's, but the gesture was comforting just the same.

Candece smiled gratefully.

"Tony, do you think anyone has figured out we're not where we're supposed to be?" A soft voice came from the far end of the raft. Tia's dark eyes shone with fear as she looked to Tony for an answer.

"If they haven't yet, they will soon. Registration ended at ten o'clock this morning. The camp director should be

contacting the school to see why we haven't checked in yet."
Tony answered, trying to make his voice sound more confident
than he really felt.

"I think we should pray." Tia's voice trembled.

"Good idea, Tia." Candece agreed, a smile instantly
appearing on her face.

"What's a good idea?" Ryan asked sleepily. He sat up and
Candece put her arm around him, hugging him as much for her
own comfort as for his.

"You're right, Tia. We should pray." Tony said, bowing his
head. He waited until the others followed his example before
beginning. "Father God, we thank You for keeping us safe and
we thank You, Father God, that we were able to find a way off
of the plane. We pray, Father God, that You will just be with
our friends and family who are still on the plane. Watch over
them, Father God, and protect them. And, Father God, we just
pray right now that You will be with us and help us to have
patience, Father God. Guide us and direct us to land quickly,
Father God, so that we will be able to rescue our friends as
soon as possible. And, Father God, just put Your hand on Mr.
Brendan, Father God. Just touch him right now. We love You
so much, Father God, and we give You all of the glory. In
Your Son's precious name, Amen."

Reese hugged Tony tightly. Anyone close to him knew that his stress level could be measured by the number of times he used the phrase "Father God."

*   *   *

"I wonder what the others are doing right now." Nat wondered out loud, breaking the monotony of silence that had covered the plane for almost an hour.

"Probably the same thing we're doing," José answered with an annoyed sigh. "Patiently waiting for something to happen."

"Do you think they've found that resort place yet?" Tommy asked, not directing his question to anyone in particular.

"Maybe." Arisa looked around at the other students sitting around the plane, leaning back against the cool metal walls. "Rescuers could even be on their way."

Everyone fell silent again.

"They're having chapel at school today." Nat said suddenly.

Arisa nodded. She couldn't believe that they'd left their school just yesterday. It seemed like years had passed since she'd been home, not just a little over twenty-four hours. She sighed as she shifted positions. She'd hardly moved since she had awakened several hours before. Her muscles ached and protested the movement.

"We could have our own little service right here." Twila exchanged a look with Nat.

"Why would we want to do that?" José was angry. "God's forgotten us out here."

"José, no." Arisa shook her head, surprised at how sure and calm her voice sounded. "He hasn't forgotten us. And it's a good idea. I think it'll make us feel better and keeping busy will make the time go faster."

"I saw a Bible over there last night." Luke pointed to one of the piles of junk.

"I'll get it." Twila got to her feet.

Arisa stopped her sister when she walked by. "Thank you, Twila. I hadn't – there was – I couldn't think of what to do next. I – just, thanks."

Twila smiled, embarrassed but savoring her sister's praise. Arisa watched the girl cross to where Luke had pointed. After a moment, she straightened. When she turned, Arisa felt her heart leap. Twila held a familiar-looking book. She handed the Bible over to her older sister without a word.

Arisa caressed the soft leather, taking a moment to enjoy having her book back. "We all know that back at school our friends are having chapel; probably praying for us." Arisa swallowed hard. "I think we should do what Twila and Nat suggested and have a time of prayer and Bible reading. You don't have to, but I think it will help us all feel better." All of the students gathered around Arisa, some hesitant, but all willing. They knew that if they were going to get through this, they needed something bigger than themselves.

"Could I read something?" Will asked.

Arisa handed her Bible over.

After a minute or so, Will cleared his throat and began to read, tentative at first, his voice growing stronger as he continued. "I think this is appropriate and it's always been one of my favorites. It's from Hebrews. '…he has said, "I will in no way leave you, neither will I in any way forsake you." So that with good courage we say, "The Lord is my helper. I will not fear. What can man do to me?"'"

"Thank you, Will." Arisa gave him a warm smile, which he returned. She paused, looking around at the rest of the group. "Anyone else?"

Twila reached for Arisa's Bible and immediately opened it to what she wanted. "This is from Psalm thirty-seven. 'Trust in Yahweh, and do good. Dwell in the land, and enjoy safe pasture. Also delight yourself in Yahweh, and he will give you the desires of your heart. Commit your way to Yahweh. Trust also in him, and he will do this: he will make your righteousness go forth as the light, and your justice as the noon day sun. Rest in Yahweh, and wait patiently for him.' I think if we focus on what we have going for us, getting through this will be easier." Twila flushed and she looked down as she continued. "Sometimes remembering that there's more to life than what's here can make all of the difference."

Arisa felt a surge of pride in her little sister. Twila wasn't one to share spiritual things with ease, especially in front of a large group.

"I have a favorite verse." Nat held out her hand. Twila passed the Bible and Nat turned a few pages. She read: "'Be still and know that I am God… Yahweh of Armies is with us. The God of Jacob is our refuge.'"

"Thanks, Nat." Arisa received her Bible once more. "This is my favorite verse. It's from Romans. 'Who shall separate us form the love of Christ? Could oppression, or anguish, or persecution, or famine, or nakedness, or peril, or sword? …No, in all these things, we are more than conquerors through him who loved us. For I am persuaded, that neither death, nor life, nor angels, nor principalities, nor things present, nor things to come, nor powers, nor height, nor depth, nor any other created thing, will be able to separate us from the love of

God, which is in Christ Jesus our Lord.' We need to remember that even if we think we're in a lot of trouble and it doesn't feel like God's here, He is and He's looking out for us." She shut her Bible and set it aside. "I think now would be a good time to pray. If anyone doesn't want to pray with us, you don't have to." No one moved. When they returned home, they might go back to scorning Christianity, but, for now, they clung to what they'd been brought up knowing.

"Let's join hands and make a prayer circle." Twila suggested the common way of praying in the youth group she and several of the other students attended. The familiarity was as welcome as the physical contact.

Arisa took Twila's and Will's hands in her own, waiting for a moment until everyone else joined hands. "If you want to pray out loud, go ahead, but don't feel like you have to. I'll close when we're done." Taking a deep breath to focus, Arisa closed her eyes and bowed her head. The others followed her example, some preparing their hearts for prayer, others merely finding solace in the ritual.

"Lord," Nat was the first to speak, waiting only a few moments. She spoke softly, nervous about praying in front of the others. She only uttered a few sentences, but her heart was sincere. "Please help us and the others to get out of here safely.

Protect them from any harm. And, Lord, help them to get back here for us quickly. And let Mr. Brendan be okay. Amen."

Will picked up as Nat's prayer ended, his calm, deep voice reassuring those around him as they heard his faith in every word. "God, we praise You for helping us so far by letting us find the raft and having us land on this sandbar so the plane isn't sinking. I just want to ask You to continue to watch over us and protect us. Be with us through the rest of this. Give us Your peace and Your joy. Help us to be loving to each other and watch over each other. Be with our friends right now and watch over them. Touch Mr. Brendan, Father, and heal him. In Your Son's name, Amen."

One by one, others began to pray. Some only offered one sentence and others poured their hearts out for twenty minutes. A spirit of peace had settled over the group, banishing their surroundings from their minds. Twila gave a short prayer of praise for keeping them safe and then asked God to watch over their friends.

The kids sat in silence for several minutes but Arisa didn't speak, sensing that she needed to wait. Then, Nat began to sing, her sweet voice carrying the simple tune. The others joined in after a few lines. They didn't know if they sounded good and they didn't care. Arisa smiled as she listened to the last few notes fading back into stillness. Everyone sat silently, worshiping God in his or her own quiet ways.

After an unknown amount of time passed, Arisa closed in prayer. "Dear God, I know You are here, and I thank You for that. Thank you for Your reminder that You're never going to leave us. I pray, Lord Jesus, You will be with each one of us as well as those of our group who left. Protect us all. I also pray You will comfort the families of those who have lost a child, brother, or sister because of this crash. Be with Mr. Brendan, God; just touch him right now. Bring comfort to each of us, God. Bring us peace so we might be reassured that You're caring for us right now and for our friends as well. I pray that everything that happens will be according to Your will and will bring glory to Your name. I'm laying down everything at Your feet, God and leaving it there. I love You. Amen."

A few echoed Arisa's final word as they raised their heads. Many wiped at tear-stained faces unashamedly, most smiling through their tears.

A weight seemed to have been lifted off of the plane but some of the kids would stay quiet for only so long.

"So, what are we going to do now?" Kris asked the question.

"What else? Talk. It's not like we can play basketball."

Twila grinned. "Besides, might be a nice way to get to know each other better."

"Good idea, Twila. Why don't you start?" Twila gave her sister a dirty look. Arisa smiled and held up an imaginary microphone. In a cheesy announcer voice, she said, "Twila McDonald, tell us a little about yourself."

After rolling her eyes, Twila leaned forward and spoke into her sister's hand. "I just came to Wycliffe Christian this year. Before here, I went to Wycliffe Middle School. There's Arisa, then me, and then we have a ten year-old sister and a brother who's seven. They both still go to Wycliffe Public. This year, our whole family will be getting together for a family reunion during Thanksgiving back at our grandparents' house in Spring Arbor, Michigan." She leaned back against the wall of the plane.

"So there's just the four of you?" Will asked.

"No. We have a younger brother who's not in school yet; he's only four. I bet Ty's missing us really bad. He didn't want us to leave. And Josie is the sweetest girl. And Oliver's so sensitive and kind." Twila glanced at Arisa. Both girls had tears in their eyes.

Luke decided to break the tension. "Do you have a boyfriend?"

Twila looked up, startled by the question. She blushed and answered, "no."

"What about pets? Do you guys like animals?" Will spoke up, wanting to save Twila from further embarrassment.

She shot him a grateful look. "Yes. I love animals. Everyone in our family does. We have two dogs, three rabbits, five horses and seven cats."

"That's almost as many animals as I have!" Luke exclaimed. He began to count on his fingers. "I have two dogs, three horses, four rabbits, seven chickens, six cats and a goat named Buster."

"A goat named Buster?" José asked.

"Long story." Kris interjected.

"Any brothers and sisters?" Nat asked Luke.

"I'm an only child." Luke said. "Kris is too."

"How long have the two of you been best friends?" José put his arm around Nat and pulled her close.

Luke and Kris exchanged looks and Kris shrugged. "I don't really know. We've been friends for as long as I can remember."

"Tony and I have known each other since fifth grade. We've had almost every class together since then." Arisa glanced towards the door of the plane as she spoke.

Will leaned over, "he'll be okay, Arisa." He put a hand on Arisa's shoulder.

"Thanks, Will." Arisa put her hand over Will's. He flushed and she looked away, pretending not to notice.

"Randy, Tammy and I have known each other for ten years." Tommy spoke up. "We even go to the same church."

Over the next few hours, the conversation shifted from the whole group talking to a few people breaking off into smaller groups as the kids discovered things they had in common. Will and Arisa sat back at first, watching the groups converse until Nat and José came over to talk with them.

"I think it's really brave that you volunteered to stay here, Arisa." Nat said.

"Thanks, Nat." Arisa said. "It was really brave of you two to volunteer to stay with us."

"It was the least we could do." José squeezed Nat's hand.

"Hey, Nat, José, we found some cards." Twila called from where she was sitting with Luke and Kris. "Do you guys want to play the Rat Game with us?"

"Sure. Come on, José." Nat stood and tugged José after her, flashing a brilliant smile back at Will and Arisa before joining her friends. Soon, laughter echoed off the cabin walls.

As the game moved faster and the kids got louder, Arisa

turned to Will. "So, how do you like WCS so far?"

"It's really great." Will answered, meeting Arisa's eyes for only a second before looking away, a red flush staining his neck and cheeks.

Arisa suppressed a smile. He was so shy. She tried to put him at ease. "You're a junior, right?" He nodded. "I thought Mrs. McKennedy said you were fifteen."

"I started school young. My birthday's in September but my parents didn't want me to wait a year to start school." Will explained. "I'll turn sixteen not long after we get back. I've always been the youngest in my class."

"Your birthday's in September?" Arisa asked. "Then you're only a month younger than me. I've always been the youngest, too. Well, until now."

"When's your birthday?" Will asked. He appeared to be relaxing as he and Arisa talked.

"August seventeenth." Arisa replied. "What day's yours?"

"The seventeenth. I guess that makes you exactly a month older than me."

Arisa smiled. "So, are you the oldest kid?"

Will nodded. "Yeah. It's me, then Candece, Ryan and..." He stopped. A pained look passed over his face.

"Will?"

Will didn't look at her as he spoke. His voice was tight, as if it might break. "Leesha. She was three years younger than Ryan. She died four years ago this past summer."

"I'm sorry," Arisa put her hand on his arm. "I didn't know."

"I know." Will looked up. "We don't talk about her a lot. It still hurts my parents too much." Will stared at the wall behind Arisa. "We were on vacation in California. At the beach. We were all swimming and then she wasn't there..."

"Will," Arisa felt her eyes filling with tears.

He looked at her, his own eyes wet. "That's why I came this week. To make sure nothing happened to my brother and sister. My parents can't handle losing another child. I don't think anyone could. Mom wasn't going to let Candece or Ryan come, but I convinced her that if I went with them, everything would be okay. And now, because of me, they might lose all of us."

"It's not your fault." Arisa surprised herself at the intensity in her voice. "None of this is your fault. And your parents aren't going to lose anyone else. We are going to be okay."

*　　*　　*

"I'm worried about Tommy." Tammy's voice quivered as

she leaned against her brother. Randy put his arm around Tammy but didn't say anything.

"My brother will take care of Tommy." Candece said confidently. "He's good at taking care of people."

"Thanks, Candece." Randy gave the young woman as much of a smile as he could muster.

"Why don't we play a game to pass the time?" Tony suggested, hoping to distract the students from their current circumstances. "It'll be fun." He tried coaxing them.

"Let's play Truth and Consequence." Reese suggested.

"What's that?" Ryan asked.

"It's a game we play at our church camp." Tony handed off his paddle to Randy who began rowing while Tony explained the game. "Kind of an icebreaker version of Truth and Dare. One person starts by asking a question. Usually something about a favorite movie or how many brothers and sisters. If the person refuses to answer or the questioner thinks the person is lying, they have to do something silly like clucking like a chicken. It's a good idea, Reese. I'll start. Tia, who's your favorite musical artist?" Tony asked.

Tia flushed. "I like Deacon 'D' Biggs. He' hot."

"He is." Reese sent a sly wink to the younger girl as Tony feigned annoyance.

Tia giggled at her counselors. "Okay, my turn." She looked at Candece. "Since you're a new kid, I'll pick you. Tell us about your best friend."

"Actually, my best friend is my pen pal from New York." Candece said shyly. "His name's Nash White and he's twelve years old."

"How'd you meet someone in New York?" Reese asked.

"We started writing through our youth groups and really hit it off. He's really nice. He comes from a huge family. He's got a bunch of older sisters and an older brother named Taylor."

"Have you ever met him in person?" Tia asked.

Candece shook her head. "Not yet, but we're going to go visit his family next summer." She thought for a moment before taking her turn. "Um, Reba, what do you like to do for fun?" Candece asked.

Everyone but Ryan and Candece groaned. Even the teachers at WCS knew the Jones girls were boy-crazy.

Reba grinned. "Check out guys of course."

Reba turned her attention to Reese. "Reese, where was you and Tony's first kiss?"

"After out third date when he took me home. We were on my porch." Reese answered readily. "My tu..."

"No it wasn't." Tony interrupted. "I kissed you while we

were dancing on our third date. A couple of hours before I took you home."

The kids snickered as Reese turned red.

"Nice to know it was memorable." Tony said wryly.

"I guess it's your turn." Reese muttered.

Tony gave Reese's shoulder a squeeze as he directed his question to Randy. "What's the strangest excuse you've given a girl for not calling her?"

"I told one girl I was washing my goldfish." Randy admitted. The girls glared at him and he immediately defended himself. "She proposed to me after having known me for ten minutes and cried when I said no. We were only ten and I was scared."

"I had a guy tell me his hamster died and they were having a funeral so he could get out of meeting my parents." Reese glanced sideways at Tony, a smile playing across her lips.

"Hey, we really did bury Sparky!" Tony said indignantly.

Everyone laughed as the two quibbled for a few moments before returning to the game. Randy turned his question to Candece. "What's your favorite movie?"

"*A Day Older*." Candece promptly replied.

"Is that the one about the newspaper kids in New York?" Tammy asked. "Those guys are totally hot and the story is way cool."

"I like that movie too." Reba agreed and Melanie nodded as well.

"The book was better." Twila chimed in.

"Always is." Arisa smiled in agreement.

"Did I ever tell any of you guys the story about my great-great-great grandparents?" Tony asked suddenly.

The kids shook their heads, not understanding the connection.

Reese looked over at Tony. "What about them?"

Tony explained. "It was back in like the early 1900s in New York City. My great-great-grandfather's dad was in prison and his mom was dead. His name was Antony Machelli and he had to work to get money for food and stuff. The only thing he could do was work as a newsie."

"Your great-great-great grandfather was a newsie?" Reba exclaimed. "That's so cool."

"Yeah, he was. And that's how he met my great-great-great grandmother. She'd come over from Ireland on a boat with her father."

"You're Irish?" Reese raised her eyebrows.

"Kinda." Tony replied. "She's like the only one not Italian in my family, so I guess I'm an eighth Irish or something like that. Anyway, her name was Belinda O'Donnell. When she got over here, her dad was sick, so immigration sent him back to Ireland, leaving her in America by herself. Because a woman couldn't really get a job or be safe on her own, she cut her hair really short and called herself Billie. She met Antony and he got her a job as a newsie. Eventually, he found out she was a girl and they fell in love. I'm named after him."

"I have a question." Ryan spoke up.

"What's that?"

"If Antony's last name was Machelli, how'd your last name get to be Vumeccelli? Or was it a marriage thing?"

"Actually," Tony grinned. "That's another story. Billie and Antony's first kid, Vincent, who was my great-great grandfather, was a bit of a troublemaker. They moved out west to get land and Vincent ended up having to move to California because he got into so much trouble. He changed his last name to Vumeccelli. Think about it. V Machelli, Vumeccelli. Sounds a lot alike and since they didn't really know how to spell too well, it got changed around. When my great grandfather came back east, he just kept the changed name."

"What did he do?" Candece asked.

"Vincent was in love with some big shot politician's daughter; or so the story goes. It was a total Romeo and Juliet thing. Only, instead of them both ending up dead, Vincent got caught in a trap set by the girl's father. It turned into a 'him-or-me' gunfight and Vincent won. He and the girl took off together."

Tammy sighed. "That's so romantic." Suddenly, a mischievous grin spread across the girl's face. "Speaking of romance, Reese, do you and Tony have any pet nicknames for each other?"

Reese blushed and Tony chuckled. She muttered, "Pickle."

"What was that?" Tia asked, not sure she heard correctly.

"I call her Pickle." Tony answered for Reese.

"Why?" Tammy asked.

"I like pickles." Reese answered.

"Well, that's not exactly the whole story." Tony spoke up. Reese glared at him, but he continued. "On our first date, we went out to this fancy restaurant. It had taken me two months to get a reservation. We got in there, and Reese ordered a glass of water, nothing more. I kept asking her why she wasn't eating anything but she wouldn't answer me. Finally, I was getting really mad and she knew it, so she told me why she wasn't eating. She'd eaten two whole jars of dill pickles before our date."

"Two jars?" Tammy exclaimed. Everyone looked at Reese.

"I was nervous." Reese said between gritted teeth, her face bright red. "At least I had enough money to cover the bill."

Everyone laughed as Tony opened his mouth and closed it again, at a loss for words. He joined in the laughter and Reese continued the game. As the afternoon sun shone down on them, the rolling waves and warm sun gently rocked the lost students to sleep. Several hours passed before anyone woke.

"Hey, Tony! Wake up!" Ryan shook Tony awake.

"What's wrong, Ryan?" Tony mumbled sleepily as he rolled over, rocking the raft. The sudden motion threw Ryan off balance and he fell back against Candece, waking her.

"There's land!" Ryan's exclamation woke the others.

"Where?" Tony suddenly sat up straight, bumping Reese. She grabbed Tony's arm to steady herself as the raft rocked dangerously.

"What's going on, Tony?" Reese asked, her grip on Tony's arm tightening.

The other students started scrambling into sitting positions.

"Look!" Reba pointed out across the ocean. A dark shadow rose from the water. The sunset cast an eerie glow across the faces of the students, shadowing them with a reddish stain.

"Randy, grab that paddle." Tony picked up the paddle near him and the two boys began to row, muscles straining to move the raft along.

The dark shadow rapidly grew closer and soon formed into a more substantial shape. The welcomed sound of sand scraping the bottom of the raft greeted the kids' ears. When the water was a little over ankle-deep, they jumped out of the raft and ran up onto the shore. Only Tony and Randy remained behind.

"Hello! We need help!" Tony yelled as he and Randy dragged the raft up onto higher ground. Mr. Brendan lay at the bottom, still unconscious.

"Is anyone here?" Reese called out as she followed the kids to the shore.

"Hello?" Reba began shouting. "Is there anyone here? We need some help! Someone please answer!"

All of the kids joined, looking and listening for a sign – any sign – of life. Only after the sun had sunk well below the horizon and dusk began to settle over the island, they finally stopped, sinking to the sand in defeat.

"There's no one here." Tia whispered, tears in her eyes.

"We know that!" Tony yelled, frustrated. He buried his head in his hands.

Shocked quiet fell, silencing the nervous chatter. All eyes turned towards Tony.

Taking a deep breath, Tony looked up at Tia and spoke in a softer tone. "I'm sorry, Tia. I was upset and shouldn't have yelled at you." He raked a hand through his hair.

"It's okay." Tia leaned against Renae who put a comforting arm around the older girl.

Tony walked over and put a hand on Tia's shoulder, apologizing again.

"This isn't where we were supposed to land on, is it?" Tammy leaned against her brother, both looking to Tony for answers.

"No, it isn't." Tony answered in a near whisper. Reese laid a hand on Tony's back. "The resort was on the east bank."

"Now what are we going to do?" Candece spoke timidly, afraid that Tony might yell at her.

"We have to go back and get the others." Randy answered. "We can't let them stay there. If we do, the plane might sink."

"He's right, Tony. We need to get the others." Reese reached for Tony's hand.

"Okay." Tony set his jaw determinedly. "I need one more person to come with me so we can take turns rowing. We'll get to the plane a lot faster. Who's coming with me?"

"I am." Reese spoke up quickly, squeezing Tony's hand and moving closer to him.

"You can't." Tony reminded her gently. "You have to stay with the kids."

"I'll go." Randy volunteered. "I couldn't stay here knowing I could have helped."

"Thanks, Randy. We'll leave first thing in the morning. It's not going to do us any good if we leave now and get lost in the dark." Tony explained. "We can sleep here tonight. Tomorrow, while Randy and I go get the others, you can make some shelter for Mr. Brendan. Make sure he gets some water every couple of hours. Let's get him out on dry land and get to sleep so Randy and I can get an early start in the morning."

*   *   *

"They're going to be okay." Will tried to put Arisa at ease. She hadn't said anything about the others over the past few hours, but she kept stealing glances at the door and he knew what – who – she was looking for.

Arisa nodded, not trusting her voice enough to speak. She chewed on her lip, struggling to control her feelings. Will sat quietly, watching Arisa as he waited for her to speak. Finally, she whispered, "I'm so scared, Will. I feel like everything is falling apart around me, like I have nothing to hold on to."

"God's still here, Arisa. I know it feels like He isn't, but He is." Will's voice was soft, comforting. He reached out a hand to touch Arisa, but stopped and pulled his hand back.

"I know." Arisa agreed. "My heart knows it, but my mind doesn't want to believe it." She fell silent.

Will sat behind her, not knowing what to say. He met her eyes and saw the helplessness he felt mirrored in her eyes.

"Arisa, come join us!" Twila called to her sister.

Arisa wiped her eyes with the back of her hand and gave Will a watery smile. He smiled back and followed her to the rest of the group.

"We're going to play Truth and Consequence." Nat said with a grin. "One of us will start by asking someone a question. If you don't want to answer or we think you're lying, you have to face the consequences."

"What are those?" Will asked warily.

Arisa tried to put him at ease. "Usually it's something like having to sing a silly song or do a goofy dance. Stuff like that. We play it at church camp all the time."

"How about someone else gets to tell an embarrassing or funny story about the person?" Kris suggested.

"Great idea!" Luke agreed and the others nodded.

"Who's going to start?" José asked.

"Twila, since it was her idea." Nat said.

"Hmm." Twila thought for a moment. "Luke, who's your favorite athlete?"

Kris snickered and Luke shot him a dirty look before answering. "Kross Midland, the snowboarder."

"Liar!" Kris shouted before Luke finished. "It's Branigan Whit."

"Shut up!" Luke snapped.

"I love Branigan Whit." Twila offered. "He's very good."

"But he's an ice skater." Kris was laughing so hard his face had turned red.

"And a black belt in karate." Nat retorted.

"He could kick your butt." José remarked to Kris.

"Besides, who says ice skating's wimpy? I happen to think it's kinda... hot." Twila smiled, winking at her sister.

Arisa smirked and managed to keep from laughing. It was a well-known WCS secret that Luke and Kris had had both had crushes on Twila since they first met her at one of Arisa's soccer games a few years ago. Faithful puppies had nothing on those two.

"You do?" Luke's eyes were wide and Kris stopped laughing. They started at Twila, openmouthed as the rest of the group found themselves doubled over with laughter.

"Kris, it's your turn." Twila said after she caught her breath.

"Okay." Kris rubbed his hands together and looked around. "Nat, was José the first guy you'd ever kissed?"

"No." Nat giggled. "When I was six, I chased a boy around the playground and kissed him." Nat turned to Arisa, curious about the upperclassman's little-known dating habits. "What about you, Arisa? Who was the first guy you kissed?"

Arisa answered without hesitation or embarrassment. "I haven't."

"You're sixteen and never been kissed?" Tommy chuckled. "I thought that was just a title of some cheesy chick movie."

"I've never kissed anyone either." Will spoke up.

"Me either." Twila admitted, flushing slightly.

"Why not?" Kris asked, puzzled.

Will and Twila looked to Arisa to answer first since it had been her question.

Arisa thought carefully before answering, trying to decide how to word what she wanted to say. "I read this book that changed the way I looked at dating. I don't want to date just anyone. I decided that if I had enough faith in God to believe He could save me from hell, then I could trust He'd take care that stuff too. God'll let me know when the time comes."

All eyes turned toward Will.

"I haven't found the right girl." Will said softly. "It's not worth wasting my time on someone who's wrong for me." He glanced at Arisa and then looked back down at his hands. "I read that book, too. That guy had some really good ideas."

"I'm not ready for a serious relationship and if a kiss is just some physical thing, what's the point?" Twila lift her head, the spark in her eyes daring anyone to make fun of her. "And, I agree with Arisa and Will. I believe God's powerful enough to make sure the right guy finds me; if He wants me married at all."

"A friend of mine is nineteen, and she still hasn't kissed anyone." Arisa said.

"You've got to be kidding me." Kris said.

"Eliana?" Twila asked.

Arisa nodded. "Her name's Eliana Sanford. She and I went to church together for thirteen years. We're best friends. She went to Kent State instead of Galludet University. She's deaf, but she never had interpreters go with her because she hated people treating her funny because she was deaf. She told me that was why we were best friends. I learned to sign so I could talk to her, but I never acted weird or treated her like she was stupid."

"Arisa taught a bunch of us some sign language." Twila

added.

"I learned ASL about a year ago." Will said. "We had a deaf woman come to my church back home and offer classes. I don't know a whole lot, but enough to carry on a conversation. I've always wanted to learn more. Does Eliana still go to your church?" He asked Arisa.

Arisa's face fell. "No, she moved to California over the summer."

"Oh, sorry." Will apologized.

"It's okay," Arisa said. "It's my turn now and we'll get on to something lighter." Her eyes moved around the circle and came to rest on one of the students. "Tommy, what's the strangest Halloween costume you've ever worn?"

"I wore a ballerina costume for Halloween when I was three." He shook his head. "I let my older cousins dress me."

"That's nothing. There's this *Hello Kitty* t-shirt...." Whatever else Kris was going to say was cut off by a strange screech from Luke as he lunged for his friend. After a brief and mild scuffle, the kids returned to their game.

"All right, Kris." Tommy turned. "What's the craziest thing you've ever done?"

"That's easy." Kris said. "I wanted to be the baby in our living Nativity at church but everyone said I was too old. I climbed in the manger and scared everyone."

"He's been banned from all church plays." Luke laughed.

"How old were you?" Nat asked between giggles.

"It was last Christmas." Luke burst out.

"Luke hid in a piano during an overnighter and fell asleep." Kris shouted, not to be outdone. "He didn't wake up until the pianist came up front to start playing for the morning service."

Everyone was in tears, barely able speak through their laughter. The two boys continued to keep everyone near hysteria and in forgetfulness for the next few hours, trying to outdo each other with completely outrageous stories.

Later, when the plane was dark, the fears they'd all been trying to hide began to surface. Arisa and Will tried to reassure the kids with hollow promises they weren't sure they themselves totally believed. Judging by the looks in the students' eyes, they didn't either.

"You can go to sleep, Will. I'm going to stay up for a little while." Arisa said softly. She didn't look at Will, not wanting him to see the tears shining in her eyes.

"Are you sure?" Will asked, concern in his voice.

Arisa nodded. She heard Will lay down behind her. Only when she thought he was asleep did she allow herself to release the tears she'd been holding all day.

Will lay still, breathing even and deep. His eyes remained open, watching Arisa as she watched over the others. Until Arisa slept, Will would stay awake.

*   *   *

The sun appeared over the horizon, casting its warming rays down on the sleeping students. Tony stirred as the sun's heat reached him through the heavy layer of fog blanketing the island. He yawned and stretched his aching limbs. Reese stirred from where she was sleeping behind him.

"Time to wake up, Reese." Tony murmured, turning over and gently shaking his girlfriend.

"Hmm?" Reese slowly opened her eyes. She sat up, wincing as her sore muscles screamed. "Why don't you wake up Randy?" She shook sand from her hair, grimacing at the gritty strands.

Tony nodded and held out a hand.

"Sure, Tony." Reese was still blinking the sleep out of her eyes as she took his hand and let Tony pull her to her feet. She squeezed his hand before he pulled it away.

Tony walked over to where Randy slept and shook the younger boy awake. "Randy, it's time to wake up. We have to get going." He kept his voice low as he spoke, not wanting to wake anyone else.

"Okay, Tony." Randy muttered, sitting up. He grimaced and rubbed the back of his hand across his face. After a moment, he got to his feet and walked with Tony to the raft.

Reese followed the boys as they pulled the raft to the water's edge. With a grunt, the boys shoved the raft part of the way into the water.

"You get in first." Tony told Randy and the young man immediately complied.

Tony leaned over and lightly kissed Reese on the lips before shoving the raft back into the cool saltwater. Once the raft was far enough out, he climbed in. He turned to wave before he and Randy picked up the paddles and began to row toward the rising sun. Soon, the pair disappeared from sight.

Reese watched long after they'd gone.

*   *   *

"Reese," Candece timidly approached her counselor, "don't you think we should pray?"

For hours, Reese had been sitting and staring out at the dark water while the younger students around her had watched, not knowing what else to do. Some of the students had managed to get Mr. Brendan to drink some of their bottled water, but he still hadn't opened his eyes. As time passed and nothing changed, their fear grew, but Reese did nothing.

"Why?" Reese snapped at the younger girl, tears brimming in her eyes. "God put us out here in the middle of nowhere! What good has He done us?!"

"Reese, He's given us a lot. We landed on a sandbar and didn't sink; we found the raft and dry land. We have a lot to be thankful for." Renae knelt at Reese's side.

"Listen, I don't care what you do. Just don't do it around me. If you'll feel better and quit whining, then go pray!" Reese turned her back to the girls and continued staring out at the ocean.

Candece looked at Renae, eyes wide. Renae shrugged her shoulders, not knowing what to do anymore than Candece did. Candece took a deep breath and approached the other kids with her idea of prayer. They welcomed it warmly, thankful for something familiar. Renae suggested that someone recite a favorite Bible verse. After a moment, Candece spoke up. "'We know that all things work together for good for those who love God, to those who are called according to his purpose… What then shall we say about these things? If God is for us, who can be against us.'" Candece paused.

Reese had come up behind the group, fresh tears streaming down her cheeks. "I am so sorry Candece, Renae, all of you. Can you forgive me?" Reese knelt in the sand between the two girls. Candece and Renae wrapped their arms around Reese as she sniffled and hugged them back. "Now, does anyone else want to say something before we pray? Then I think we should make some kind of shelter for Mr. Brendan."

"I have a verse." Ryan spoke up. "'You are of God, little children, and have overcome them; because greater is he who is in you than he who is in the world... For whatever is born of God overcomes the world. This is the victory that has overcome the world: your faith.'"

*   *   *

Evening had come and Arisa and her group were once again sharing the things that made up their lives. They were enjoying the discussions, finding more in common with their schoolmates than they'd previously thought possible.

"Kris, what were you going to Camp Ventner for?" Twila asked.

"Art." Kris said with a mixture of embarrassment and pride.

"He's an awesome artist." Luke immediately praised his friend.

"Have you every talked to Tony about drawing?" Arisa asked. Kris shook his head. "You should. He's really good. He used to draw comics of our class. Thought about doing it professionally, but decided he liked medicine more."

"Oh, Arisa, I heard a rumor Tony gave you some nickname after a chipmunk or something like that?" Tommy asked.

Twila snickered.

Arisa chuckled and rolled her eyes. "Yeah. Once when Eliana came to a basketball game, the two of us got laughing really hard and Tony said we were nuttier than chipmunks. So he started calling me Dale and Eliana was Chip. Like from the old cartoon..."

A loud shout from outside interrupted her story. "Hey! Anyone in there?"

Arisa stood up and ran to a window, hope filling her. "It's Tony and Randy!" She yelled, excitement filling her voice. Her whisper was lost in the cheers of the kids behind her. "Thank You, God!" She flung open the door, letting in the fading sunlight.

Will tapped Arisa on the shoulder and handed her some clothes he and Twila had tied together, making a crude rope.

Arisa took it and tossed it to Tony who caught it and tied the end to a small loop at the end of the raft.

That being done, the pair climbed into the plane; the motion of the raft on the waves made it difficult to move quickly, but they hurried nonetheless. The students met the two young men with much enthusiasm and warm hugs. Randy smiled and accepted the hugs, but it was obvious the young man was embarrassed by all of the attention. Tony just smiled and enjoyed it. But after a few minutes, he made his way to Arisa's side.

"Arisa, I have to talk to you. Right now." The urgency in Tony's voice was evident only to Arisa as he kept a fake smile plastered on his face. Tony took his friend aside and talked to her quietly, telling her everything that had happened since he'd left. When he was done, Arisa didn't say anything. It was almost a full minute before she regained her voice.

*   *   *

"I can't believe it." Arisa kept her voice down so the others wouldn't hear. She shook her head and sighed. "Lord, why?" She whispered the words, closing her eyes. She didn't know what to do. She'd been so sure that once Tony reached land, everything would be okay. He would send a rescue crew and they would all go home. She hadn't let herself ask why he and Randy had come back instead of sending someone. Now she knew why.

"We have to hurry." Will interrupted. His voice was controlled, but Arisa read the tension on his face. "The waves are getting rougher. I think we better move right now."

Will looked at Arisa, an unasked question about the anxiety on her face written in his eyes. She shook her head, "not now."

"Okay, let's go." Tony glanced back at Arisa. She clenched her jaw and looked back at Tony, her gaze steady.

"All right, everyone, listen up." Arisa called. She squelched her rising panic and took a step forward. "We have to hurry. Everyone, grab whatever food is left and any clean clothes you can see."

"Why do we need clothes and food?" Will leaned over and whispered in Arisa's ear.

"Trust me, you don't want to know." Arisa muttered to him under her breath and then raised her voice so the kids could hear her. "Go line up by the door and wait there." Arisa motioned for Tony and Will to follow her.

The kids hurried to do as Arisa said, eager to leave. Most of them began talking about what they would do when they got home; a hot shower and soft bed were mentioned more than once. None of them asked why they needed the food or clothes, so preoccupied they were by the thoughts of home, but Arisa knew she'd have to tell them the truth soon. She wanted to let Will know first and told him as soon as the three had moved far enough from the students to not be overheard. He reacted better than she'd expected, nodding and setting his mouth in a firm line, ready to do what needed to be done.

"So what's the resort like?" Luke asked as he lined up by the door carrying some of his clothes and a few packages of peanuts. "Any hotels with a hot tub?"

"We didn't really see any hotels." Tony avoided looking at Luke.

"How's Mr. Brendan?" José asked.

Tony didn't answer.

"Why are we taking all of this with us?" Twila asked the question Arisa knew would be coming. Twila looked at her sister and then at Tony. Her gaze slid over to Randy and then returned to Tony. "And why did you two come back for us alone?"

"We have to tell them." Arisa said. Tony looked down at her, his dark eyes becoming darker.

"Tell us what?" Kris joined his friends.

"You're right." Tony spoke to Arisa. He sighed; his whole body sagged with exhaustion.

"Do you want to tell them or should I?" A wave of sympathy for her friend washed over Arisa.

"You do it, please." Tony was almost pleading.

Arisa nodded. She thought for a moment and decided straightforward would be the best way. "Listen up," Arisa waited for everyone's attention. "I have something important to tell you and I need everyone to listen." She paused for a moment, praying that she would choose the correct words. "The island where Tony and the others landed, as far as they can tell, isn't the right one. It's... uninhabited."

"What are you talking about?" Twila's voice was tight. It sounded like something out of a cheesy Hollywood movie.

"It's solid ground." Tony looked to Randy for help, but the young man shrugged his shoulders, not knowing what he could add. "It's safe."

"We'll just be there until someone comes to get us. It shouldn't take more than a few hours." Arisa tried to sound optimistic.

"In fact," Randy interjected. "Someone might even be there already and they're all just waiting for us to come back." He glanced at Tony and Arisa for confirmation.

"He's right." Tony agreed and Arisa nodded.

"We need to go now." Will spoke softly in Arisa's ear. He then raised his voice to address the others. "The quicker we get to the island, the quicker we can leave there and get home."

"All right, let's go!" Luke exclaimed.

"Is everyone ready?" Arisa asked.

The students answered positively. They clung to Randy's suggestion of a waiting rescue team.

The counselors walked over to the door first. Tony opened it, letting a burst of fresh air into the plane. He climbed down the plane; Randy followed close behind. Arisa tossed the clothes and bags of food down to Tony and Randy and then helped each of the students down as far as she could reach and then Tony took over. Once all of the kids were all safely in the raft, Arisa & Will climbed down and joined their friends. As Tony and Randy began to paddle away from the plane, the others turned to look at the plane.

Everything was growing dark, but an outline was still visible. As they watched, the plane rocked and its nose began to tip, slowly falling toward the water. The kids watched, mesmerized, as it slipped off the sandbar and into the dark ocean, disappearing from sight.

No one spoke. A stunned silence blanketed the kids. Tony

and Randy didn't even move to pick up their paddles. No one spoke. The gentle lapping of the water was the only sound all around them.

"I – I guess we got out of there just in the nick of time." Twila broke the silence. Her face was pale and her hands trembling. Her quiet voice sounded odd in the still, open air.

"Thank God for that." Arisa managed to keep her voice fairly steady while inwardly she was shaking as badly as her sister. She took a deep breath to calm her nerves.

Silence filled the evening air once more as Tony and Randy resumed their rowing. The rhythmic sound of paddles in the water and waves lapping against the raft almost put the kids to sleep. They sat, motionless, as everything around them faded into darkness. The kids watched the moon and stars come out, lighting the night enough so they could see the outlines of the others. Hours, or it might have been a lifetime, later, Nat voiced what all of them were thinking.

"I just want to go home." She her voice trembled as she struggled to hold back her tears.

"We all do, Nat. We all do." José put his arm around his girlfriend and pulled her close. He held her tightly and she snuggled up to him.

"Just try to go to sleep." Tony said. "Randy and I will get us to the island and we'll wake you then."

"I don't think I'm going to be able sleep, Tony." Arisa whispered to her friend, trying to convey to him some of what she was feeling, hoping that he would understand.

"I know I couldn't. That's why I'm rowing." Tony said. He threw an understanding smile over his shoulder at Arisa. "At least get some rest. You look really tired. I know you haven't gotten much sleep."

Arisa shook her head.

"Just rest. It's okay to take a break now."

"Thanks." She managed a smile. Suddenly, she sat forward. "Tony," she asked. "Do you know how to get back to the island?"

"Hey, remember who you're talking to?" Tony managed a grin. He'd had spent many years in Boy Scouts and was quite adept at finding his way around, even if he was in a strange place. More than once he'd helped a parent lost on the way to a basketball game.

"Yeah," Arisa raised an eyebrow. "I don't think ocean currents and road maps are the same thing."

"But I'm just that good." Tony's smile widened.

Arisa chuckled softly and moved to rest against the side of the raft. Abruptly, she sat forward, blushing as she realized she'd leaned back against Will.

"Are you okay?" Will asked, concern in his voice. He put a hand on Arisa's shoulder.

"I'll be fine. I was just going to... I... Tony told me to rest." Arisa explained, thankful Will couldn't see her reddened face in the darkness.

"It's okay." Will assured her. "You can lean on me. I don't mind." He gave a self-conscious smile that Arisa felt more than saw.

With a grateful look and a sigh, Arisa settled against Will's chest. The steady beat of his heart against her back soothed her. Will put his arm across the raft behind Arisa's shoulders and she rested her head on his shoulder, closing her eyes. Sleep claimed her not much later, letting her forget about her problems for at least the few hours until Randy woke them all.

"Arisa! Will! Everybody! Wake up!"

Arisa woke almost immediately but it took a moment before Arisa could see properly in the waning moonlight. All around her, the other kids were waking up, prompted by Randy's exclamation. Will stirred, causing Arisa to realize she was still leaning on him. With an embarrassed smile, she sat up, giving him room to move.

"See, it's right there." Tony pointed to a dim form in the

distance. A buzz of excitement went through the kids as they squinted at where Tony was pointing. The cloud of misery that had been hanging over the kids lifted as the island became clearer and a spirit of adventure settled on them as they grew closer to the shore, knowing that soon they would be on dry land again. Sure that their stay on the island would be short, just enough for something to talk about when they got back home, the prospect seemed exciting.

"How long until we reach it?" Twila asked.

"About ten or fifteen minutes." Tony dug deeper into the water with his paddle and encouraged Randy to do the same. The students sat forward, on edge as Randy and Tony inched the raft closer.

Arisa looked behind her, out to the east, seeing a thin sliver of pink appear over the horizon. The gray sky began to change to a faded blue as the sun rose in the cloudless morning sky, promising a clear, warm day.

Soon, the welcomed sound of sand scraping the bottom of the raft reached their ears. Randy, Tony, Will and Arisa jumped out of the raft into the ankle deep water, shivering as the cold saltwater soaked into their socks and shoes. They grabbed the sides of the raft and pulled it toward dry land. Before it was up on the shore, the students scrambled out of the raft and up the sandy beach. They sprawled on the ground, running their fingers through the fine white sand. The older teenagers sat down and took off their shoes and socks, wringing out the sopping wet material and then pulling their shoes back on.

"Where is everyone?" Luke asked.

"I thinking just landed on a different side." Tony explained. "We just need to walk the shoreline and we'll find them."

"We'll do that after we get a little sleep." Arisa looked over at Randy and Tony. Both looked exhausted. "You and Randy need to get some rest. You look like you couldn't make it half a yard. If any of the rest of you want to sleep, too, go ahead, I'll keep an eye out."

"I'll keep watch with you." Will spoke up.

"Thanks, guys." Tony's voice even sounded tired.

Arisa smiled at him and walked to the outside of the group. She sat down, facing the rising sun. Will sat next to her, but didn't speak.

"Some luck, huh?" Arisa's words were laced with unfamiliar bitterness.

"I don't know." Will shrugged. "When we get home, I'm thinking of buying a lottery ticket." One corner of his mouth tipped up in a half-smile. "Newton's law."

"I think you mean Murphy's Law. Anything that can go wrong…" Arisa let her sentence trail off.

"Nope." Will shook his head. "Newton. Every action has an opposite and equal reaction."

"I don't get it."

"If things are this bad now, how good will they get later?" Will let the smile cover his entire face.

Arisa laughed.

"Ah, success." Will brushed some sand from Arisa's arm.

"Thanks." Arisa felt her cheeks grow hot as Will's fingers came in contact with her skin.

Will dropped his hand back to his side. "But if we see a giant column of black smoke, you're on your own."

Arisa snickered again and the tension was broken. Silence fell once more as the pair watched the sun rise.

After a few hours passed, the students began to wake and get restless, wanting to get back to their friends and the rescue team who would surely be waiting. Finally, Arisa and Will agreed that they needed to wake Tony and the rest of the group. Arisa crossed to where Tony lay while Will started on the others.

Randy was already awake and pulling the raft farther up onto the beach to get it away from the tide. He left it out in the open visible to anyone flying by, but he weighted it down so the strong ocean breeze couldn't blow it away.

"What time is it?" Tony mumbled, rubbing his hand across his face.

"I don't know." Arisa looked at Will who glanced at his watch and held up a hand. "It's almost nine o'clock." She answered.

"Okay. We should get going." Tony sat up and yawned, stretching his arms into the air. He grimaced at the pain and stood, continuing to stretch out his reluctant muscles. "The rest of the group landed on the east bank of the island before. Judging from where the sun's coming up, we're to the northeast. If we head toward the sun, we should be going in the right direction." He looked at Arisa, "theoretically, anyway."

"Come on, you guys." Will was trying to coax the other students to get up. "We have to get going." He sighed as he shook Luke again.

"I guess you're right." Kris grumpily got to his feet.

"Luke, get up." Will finally just picked up the slumbering student and put him on his feet.

Luke stumbled, but stayed standing.

"Arisa, we're ready to go." Will said as everyone grabbed whatever they had carried to the raft and turned to their counselors for further instruction. Arisa looked over at Tony, waiting. He gave her a weary, pleading look and pointed in the direction they needed to go.

"Let's go." Arisa nodded and set off at a brisk pace.

The nine weary teens followed Arisa, trying to match her speed. Tony walked last, making sure no one was left behind. Will moved back and forth between Tony and Arisa, occasionally sticking with one for a short exchange before moving on again.

"Arisa, my legs hurt. Can't we take a break?" Luke complained, finally voicing to their leader what many of the other kids had been saying to each other for the past hour.

"In a few minutes." Arisa said. The cut on her cheek stung as sweat rolled over it, washing away the dirt and blood, but she still didn't stop. She forced herself to concentrate on walking rather than the millions of other thoughts bubbling inside. She poured all of her energy into pushing her exhausted body forward.

"Come on, Arisa. We're tired." Twila trotted up to Arisa's side. "We're tired and hungry. We can't keep up this pace much longer. "

"Arisa." Will reached out and touched the young woman's arm.

Arisa jumped at the contact, snapping out of her driven reverie. "Let's take a break and get something to eat and drink. Pass around the water but don't overdo it. We don't want anyone getting sick. And even if you don't feel like it, drink something. We can't risk anyone getting dehydrated." She sat down on the sand and wiped the beads of sweat off her forehead. She glanced up at the sun, now almost directly overhead and then looked back at the kids behind her as they sank gratefully to the ground.

Will sat down close to Arisa. Sensing he was watching her, Arisa turned to meet his eyes. He held her gaze for a minute and then looked away, embarrassed by his staring. Arisa continued watching him after he looked away. He absently brushed at his thick hair, pushing out of his eyes. Blood had started to seep through the crude bandage that Arisa had made for him on the plane, but it didn't appear to need immediate attention.

Will noticed Arisa looking at his arm and gave her a small smile. He handed her a bottle of water. It was warm, but wet, and Arisa drank gratefully. As the water quenched her thirst and a gentle ocean breeze cooled her, the thoughts chaotically bouncing through her head slowed. She closed her eyes and silently asked for forgiveness for her lack of patience. A

feeling of peace washed over her and a new determination set
in.

"Thank You." Arisa breathed out the prayer. She opened her
eyes and looked around with fresh eyes.

Nat and José sat together, hands linked, Nat's head resting
on her boyfriend's shoulder. Neither spoke, finding comfort
just in each other's presence. Luke and Kris were involved in a
complex conversation about a new video game they'd bought
back home. Tony and Randy sat near them, talking about
something Arisa couldn't hear. Twila watched them with an
absent look on her face, her mind obviously elsewhere.
Tommy sat by himself, staring at the ocean, thinking about
something that brought a smile to his sunburned face.

After resting for almost ten minutes, Arisa stood, picked up
her pack and said, "we should be getting to the others soon.
Let's get going." Arisa's voice was strong, but sounded forced
to her own ears. Will looked at Arisa, his eyes asking if she
wanted him to take over. She shook her head, determination
covering her fatigue. "Thanks anyway." He nodded.

Arisa waited for a minute as everyone stood and gathered
their things. She watched as the students reluctantly got to their
sore feet, wanting to find their friends and go home, but tired
of walking. They were hungry, sick of the airplane food, and

physically exhausted. They all just wanted it to be over. To be home with their families and friends. To go back to normal.

The students walked in the hot sun for two more hours, grateful that Arisa had slowed her pace to an easier one. They were almost to the point of giving up when they saw a figure jumping and waving its arms.

*   *   *

Tammy had spotted them. She jumped up and down, waving her arms, and then spun around and ran a few feet further up the beach to where Reese sat with Candece and Ryan.

"Reese! Reese!" Tammy grabbed the young woman's arm. "They're back!"

"Where?" Reese jumped to her feet and ran in the direction Tammy pointed, crossing the distance in less than a minute.

"Tony!" Reese threw her arms around Tony's neck. He smiled and wrapped his arms around her waist.

"And here I was worried you wouldn't miss me." Tony teased. He buried his face in Reese's hair as she ducked her head into his chest, arms locked in a death grip around his neck. Her tears soaked into his grubby shirt as he whispered to her. "It's okay. Shh. Everything's going to be okay." He blinked back tears of his own.

*   *   *

Arisa watched as Tammy ran toward her brother and her boyfriend, crying as she went back and forth between the two. "Randy! Tommy! I didn't know if I'd ever see you again!"

Smiling at the reunions, Arisa walked off alone. She took in the makeshift structures the kids had made from tree branches and the clothes they'd brought with them. She dropped the pack she was carrying onto the ground and sat down in the shade of one of the shelters, watching as everyone crowded around Tony and the kids, wanting to hear their stories and share their own. She saw Mr. Brandon, still unmoving, lying under the shelter next to her. He seemed to have a little more color now and she made a mental note to go with Tony and check on him later. She smiled as she watched Candece and Ryan nearly knock their brother to the ground with enthusiastic hugs. Will looked over their heads for a second to smile at Arisa before turning his attention back to his younger brother and sister. Arisa was happy this part of the journey was over, but a nagging voice in the back of her mind wouldn't let her forget the current problem. The peace she'd felt earlier was still there, but it had started to fade.

Arisa looked up. Tony had grabbed Reese's hand and was heading towards her.

He looked down at her. "I'm sorry about back there. I'm going to do more."

"Thanks, Tony." Arisa was sincerely grateful. She knew Tony and Reese wouldn't take on the full responsibility that lay ahead of them, but having their help would ease the burden from Will and her. She really couldn't put the blame entirely on them. Both had been born to privileged families and never had to worry about anything serious. Their biggest decisions were usually centered around what new stuff to buy or where to go to dinner. She'd known them both for years and had yet to see either go through anything more difficult than their respective parents' opinions of their relationship.

Tony reached out a hand to Arisa. She smiled up at him and took his hand in hers. Tony gave his friend's hand a quick squeeze. Reese wouldn't let go of Tony long enough to do the same, but she smiled widely before they walked away so Reese could show the new kids where to find fresh water.

Arisa sighed and stared out across the ocean, glancing up at the clear blue sky every few seconds, praying for any sign of rescue. After a couple of minutes, she closed her eyes and breathed out a quiet prayer. "I don't know what to do, God. I don't think I can make it through this. The only thing I know for sure is that You've promised to be there for me if I just call on You. I'm doing more than that right now, God. I'm pleading with You, begging You to help me. God, you know where we are. You're the only one who does. Please, let someone find us soon. Please tell someone where we are."

Chapter Four

"Mrs. McKennedy, there's a phone call for you on line four." The secretary's voice came over the intercom. The high school classroom was empty of students; the teacher sat at her desk, working on the lesson plans for the next week. School had let out only fifteen minutes before and the teachers were hurrying to finish their paperwork so they, too, could go home. She had almost finished when the call came.

Mrs. McKennedy closed her lesson plan book away, wondering who could be on the telephone. She never received calls at work. She pushed back her chair and sighed as she got to her feet. She walked down the hallway, deep in thought about her schedule, including having to drive to the airport with her brother to pick up the returning students. The bus driver who had driven the kids to the airport before had called a few hours ago to say his bus had broken down, so she'd spent the following half hour trying to make arrangements.

She entered the office and crossed to the phone. She pressed the button for line four and spoke. "Hello?"

"Mrs. McKennedy?" A man's deep voice came over the receiver.

"Yes? May I ask to whom I am speaking?" Mrs. McKennedy's forehead wrinkled in thought.

"I'm Mr. Albern from Camp Ventner." He sounded annoyed. "It was my understanding that nineteen students, four student counselors and four teachers were supposed to be coming from your school to my camp. Is that correct?"

"What do you mean *supposed* to be coming?" A cold hand clenched around her heart.

"I just spoke with some of my counselors and was informed that no one from your school ever got here." Mr. Albern's voice had thawed a bit.

"And you just now noticed? It's the last day of camp." Mrs. McKennedy tried to eliminate the panic from her voice and succeeded. Her anger easily covered it.

"We had another school come in at the last minute. Some things were miscommunicated and no one realized your kids weren't here. One of the counselors from another school knew one of the counselors from your school and she just mentioned to me that her friend hadn't shown up. I asked around and called you as soon as the information was confirmed." Mr. Albern hurried through his explanation, beginning to sound nervous. "None of the students or counselors from your school arrived on Monday. I called to discuss why you never called to cancel but if you didn't know they weren't here, I suggest you call the authorities."

Mrs. McKennedy's had face drained of color. She grabbed onto the desk to steady herself as she lowered herself into the chair. She didn't hear the man on the other end of the phone as she set the receiver back in its place. She buried her head in her hands, trying to sort out the confusing thoughts running through her head. Finally, she took a deep breath and tried to regain her composure as she reached for the phone. She dialed with a shaking hand.

"Chief McGinnes, please." Mrs. McKennedy asked for her old friend, voice trembling despite her efforts to control it. She fidgeted with her wedding ring, absently noticing how strange her hand looked with it rather than the engagement ring she'd worn for several years before finally getting married. She thought of her husband of three years who was away on business and quickly prayed that nothing would happen to him. Finally, she heard a familiar voice on the other end of the phone.

"Chief, this is Linda McKennedy." Mrs. McKennedy was on the brink of tears. She paused, afraid her voice would break. She waited for a moment before she continued, trying to regain her composure and figure out where to start with the bad. The chief waited patiently, knowing something was wrong.

"This past Saturday, I sent twenty-three students, ranging

from twelve to eighteen years of age, and two teachers, on a plane to go to Camp Ventner. Only four of the students were upperclassmen. The rest were junior high students and a few freshmen. I just received a phone call from the man who runs the camp. He informed me that none of my students are there; they never arrived. No one even noticed they were missing until today. One of the counselors mentioned to the director that someone she knew, a girl from my school, wasn't there so the director started asking around and found out about the missing kids. Something terrible has happened, I just know it. If there was any way to let us know what had happened, I'm sure they would have done so. Even if something had happened to Mr. Brendan and Mrs. McNeil, I'm sure Arisa or one of the other student counselors would have called. It's been four days. Where could they be? I..." The usually calm teacher was close to hysterics as the words poured from her mouth uncontrollably.

Chief McGinnes cut in. "Linda, calm down. I need to know every detail of the trip so I can find out exactly where they ended up missing."

*   *   *

"You need to call the parents right away. I don't know what you should say, but it'll be better coming from you."

They had been talking for almost twenty minutes. The chief had explained to Mrs. McKennedy exactly what he was going to do and let her ask as many questions as she needed to ask, but the time for talking was done. Action needed to be taken.

The secretary continued to watch the telephone exchange through numerous furtive looks. She knew by Mrs. McKennedy's troubled expression that something wasn't right. She'd made a phone call immediately after the cryptic call that had brought her to the office. The teacher had kept her voice hushed so that the secretary couldn't quite hear what it was the teacher was saying, although she was straining to do just that. Just before Mrs. McKennedy hung up the phone, the secretary glanced at the clock and realized she had to pick up her sons at soccer practice. She reluctantly got to her feet and pulled her purse onto her shoulder as she hurried out of the room.

*   *   *

Mrs. McKennedy took a deep breath and agreed to do what her fried had suggested. As soon as she hung up the phone, she walked went back down to her room and grabbed the folder with all of her camp information. As she walked back to the office, she opened up to her list of campers. The first name was Joseph Black.

Taking a deep breath and praying her voice wouldn't betray her, Mrs. McKennedy sat down and dialed the number listed across from the young man's name. The phone rang once, twice. Then, someone answered the other line.

"Hello, Mrs. Black?" To Mrs. McKennedy's relief, she sounded normal. "This is Mrs. McKennedy from Wycliffe Christian. I was wondering if you and your husband could come to my classroom tonight at five thirty. There's been a slight change in plans for picking up the kids."

Mrs. McKennedy listened for a moment and then answered. "No, your son hasn't done anything wrong, I just need to speak with you."

Another minute went by.

"Good. I'll see you tonight."

With a sigh, she hung up the phone. She muttered under her breath, "only thirteen more to go. Thank God we only let some of the students go. This could have been so much worse." Sighing, she continued down the list. "Okay, next is... oh, boy. The Burnetts. Oh my. We're going to have some major lawsuits coming." She rested her head in her hands. "Why did I let Reese and Tony go? Their parents are going to sue the school for everything."

*   *   *

Mrs. McKennedy took a deep breath before entering her classroom. She glanced in the window as she reached for the doorknob. The families were sitting in the classroom, worry written on every face. Concerned, most had arrived early, expecting to be the only ones there; instead, they found the room crowded with parents, stepparents, and other children.

"Good evening." She spoke as she entered the room. All eyes turned to stare at her. "Thank you for being patient with me, I had a few things I needed to check on before I could come speak with you."

She stood behind her desk, avoiding the questioning looks. After almost a full minute of silence, she forced herself to look at each person in turn, not flinching away from the confusion in his or her eyes.

"I called you all here to tell you some very difficult news. I know all of you are wondering why your children have not returned home tonight as was originally planned." She took a deep breath. "Today I received a call from the director of

Camp Ventner. He has informed me that the students we sent never reached their destination."

Parents stared at the teacher in shock as faces drained of color. Others shook their heads, in denial. One woman fainted and her husband attempted to revive her.

One set of parents were the first to their feet, shouting at the teacher as others began to raise their voices. "If anything happens to my son, we're going to sue this school..."

Another set of parents immediately yelled back. "Why isn't that a surprise?"

"Like you weren't thinking it?" The first man shot back.

"Sergio, Angelina, please." Mrs. McDonald stepped between the sets of screaming adults. "Charles, Anne, put aside your problems and let Mrs. McKennedy tell us what she knows."

The four glared at each other, and then at Mrs. McDonald, but they returned to their seats and allowed the teacher to continue speaking.

"Thank you, Mrs. McDonald. I appreciate your cooperation, Mr. and Mrs. Vumeccelli, Mr. and Mrs. Burnett." Mrs. McKennedy placed her hands on her desk to stop the shaking. "I've already contacted the police and they're looking for the kids right now. From what we've learned so far, we know that

the kids reached the airport and left on the plane. After that...
we don't know. We lost all contact with the pilot and the plane
hasn't been seen since Monday, so we don't know if anything
happened to it, and if something did... we don't know what's
happened. The two teachers with the group are missing as
well." Mrs. McKennedy took a deep breath but her voice
trembled despite her efforts. "I'm so sorry. There was no way I
could have known this was going to happen. The company I
hired to fly them out has a good reputation. I promise I will do
everything in my power to get these kids back to where they
belong – here, at home with you. I am truly sorry for all that's
happened." Mrs. McKennedy hurried through the end of her
speech, worried she might burst into tears if she talked any
longer.

"Where's Mrs. Joyce?" Mr. McDonald looked around the
room. "Shouldn't she be here?"

Mrs. McKennedy's worry was momentarily replaced by a
scowl. "I just got off the phone with Mrs. Joyce. That's why I
was late. She didn't want me to tell you any of this... for... for
PR reasons." Mrs. McKennedy's voice shook again, this time
with anger. She'd spent too much time disguising her dislike of
the current WCS principal and it was too much to continue the
charade with everything going on. "She said if I wanted to be

foolish and tell you what I knew, I'd have to do it alone."

"I have a question." Mrs. McDonald took the hand of the woman sitting next to her.

Mrs. McKennedy recognized the petite blond as the mother of the three new students who'd gone. Mr. Johnson had his arm around his wife, his face grim.

"I have two daughters... out... there. What I want to know... would anyone like to get together with my husband and me for prayer after Mrs. McKennedy finishes here?" Tears glistened in her eyes. They spilled down her cheeks as she spoke but her voice was steady. "We can meet at my house. I'll give directions to anyone who wants to come."

"We can do it here." Mrs. McKennedy offered before anyone else could speak. Her own eyes filled with tears. She struggled to hold them back but failed miserably and they ran down her face. "If anyone wants to, they can leave now. I don't have anything else to tell you. The police have everyone's numbers and they'll call as soon as they hear anything."

No one left as all eyes turned to Mrs. McDonald.

"Let's all join hands and bow our heads. We need to lift up these young people and the two teachers in prayer." Mrs. McDonald said, her voice stronger than Mrs. McKennedy would have thought possible. Mr. McDonald reached out and took his wife's hand.

All around the room, everyone joined hands and bowed their heads, forming a haphazard circle. One by one, they poured their hearts out to God. Some prayed quietly while others cried and spoke aloud, all joining together in their tragic commonality. Age, race and denominational beliefs were no longer important; all that mattered were their missing loved ones. People who hadn't prayed in years, if ever, found themselves lifting their voices.

For hours, the families and teacher of the missing petitioned God. Finally, some of the people began to look up from their prayers, faces wet with tears. They hugged and began to cry again. Then, around midnight, two stood and put on their coats, leaving the room without a word. Over the next hour, people began to follow their example, returning to their homes to wait.

Soon, only Mrs. McKennedy remained. She knelt on the floor in her classroom, pouring her heart out to God. After another hour, she finished and stood. She turned out the lights and locked the door to her room. As she walked down the dark and deserted hallway, she continued her silent prayer that had turned into a two-word plea. "Please, God."

*　　*　　*

Through the early morning hours, the word spread through everyone at Wycliffe Christian and into every church represented by the families, staff and students. Before next the day was over, hundreds of people all over the country were praying for the missing students and teachers. But, still, no word came.

*   *   *

"Arisa, can I talk to you for a minute?" Will put a hand on Arisa's arm and lead her away from the rest of group.

Everyone else was so engrossed in the story Twila was telling about her trip to the Dominican that they didn't notice the pair leave. Arisa followed Will to a shaded spot a few yards away and waited for him to speak. He held her gaze and she felt a cold hand grip her heart at the shadow she saw over his normally clear eyes.

"What is it?" Arisa tucked a strand of hair behind her ear. She wasn't sure she wanted to hear the answer.

"We don't have enough food for much longer. The food on the plane that wasn't ruined... we've been rationing it for over four days now. We only have enough to get through today."

Will spoke softly even though no one was paying attention to them. "If we don't find something to eat, we're going to have bigger trouble than we already do. Mr. Brendan's been eating and drinking a little when we force him to, but if we don't have food, I don't think he'll last much longer."

"Tony, Reese, come over here please." Arisa called to her friends who were sitting at the back of the group listening to Twila's story. They came, puzzled expressions on their faces. "Will has something to say." She glanced at Will who motioned for her to continue. He'd opened up around her but still kept to himself when Tony and Reese were around.

"What's wrong?" Reese asked, her eyes wide with concern. "Is Mr. Brendan...?"

"No, no." Arisa answered quickly and then hesitated, trying to think of some way to tell Reese and Tony the latest turn of events. She wasn't sure how they would take it. She looked to Will for help, not sure how to say what she needed to say.

"There's no food." Will got straight to the point. "We barely have enough left for today. We still have water, but eventually, we're going to need to eat."

"What are we going to do?" Reese looked to her boyfriend for an answer.

"What can we do?" Tony shrugged, completely at a loss.

"I... don't know." His gaze moved from Reese to Arisa.

"I don't know what to do either, Tony. I was hoping you would have some ideas." Arisa chewed on her bottom lip as she thought.

"Well, I think with all of these trees and bushes and stuff, there has to be some fruit or something like that somewhere." Will kept his eyes on his hands as he spoke.

"I've been thinking." Arisa said. "What if we're just too far away for someone to hear us? Maybe there are people here, just further away. I think I should check out the rest of the island."

"Not by yourself." Will immediately protested.

"Are you crazy?" Reese exclaimed. "We'll be getting rescued any minute."

"And what if we don't?" Arisa's voice was soft. She suddenly looked tired. "Reese, it's Friday. We're out of food and running out of options. Mr. Brendan is getting worse. What happens if after all we've been through, we find out there were people just a few miles away on the other side of the island? Just far enough that they haven't seen or heard us, but close enough we could reach them? I think it's worth the risk."

Tony silenced Reese's protest with a squeeze from his hand and then spoke. "I'm going to have to agree with you on this one, Arisa. If there's any possibility someone else is on this island, we have to find out. Anyone who's out looking for us might take weeks to get this far." Tony swallowed hard, forcing himself to say what the others feared. "Mr. Brendan doesn't have weeks. And, if we don't find food, neither do we. I don't think you should go alone, Arisa. Will, you should go with her. And, the two of you, only go for a day or so. If you haven't reached anyone by then, turn around and come back. If someone does happen to find us, I don't want to waste time looking for you two."

"We can leave tomorrow morning if no one's come by then." Will spoke while Arisa nodded in agreement.

Arisa added, "you know, I remember seeing some kind of berries while we were walking here." She turned to Will. "Do you think you could find them again?"

Will nodded. "I remember."

"I hadn't thought about it before, but there were a couple of apple trees further back in the woods." Reese's face brightened. She looked around outside of the shade of the tall tree where she and the others sitting. Within a few seconds, she spotted the girl and pointed. "Tia found them while you were gone. And Tammy said she and Twila had found some type of berry bush when they were out walking earlier this morning."

"Well, what are we waiting for?" Arisa got to her feet. "I'll take Twila, Randy, Tia and Tammy to go get the apples and check those berries the girls found. Will, you take José, Kris, and Luke and see if you can find those other bushes. Tony, you and Reese stay here, gather what we bring in and keep an eye on Mr. Brendan."

"Sounds good." Tony reached for Reese's hand. "Let's go."

*   *   *

"Tony, here are some apples." Arisa put down the heavy bundle. The small, tart apples rolled out onto the sand.

"Thanks." Tony dumped out the rest of the fruit and began to count.

"Is Will's group back yet?" Arisa put some of the apples into her pockets.

"Are you taking those to Mr. Brendan?" Tony asked. "He's already eaten."

"I'm taking them with me and Will. We're also going to take two of the sleeping bags." Arisa sat down next to Tony. She let out a breath and shielded her eyes from the sun as she looked around the beach, counting the students again. She couldn't relax until she was sure everyone she'd accounted for everyone.

"You don't like waiting, do you?" The edge of Tony's mouth twitched upward into the shadow of a smile. He looked up at Arisa.

"I can't take just sitting here. I feel like I should be up and doing something." Arisa lowered her voice. "If you want to know the whole truth, I just have a bad feeling about this place. The whole situation feels wrong. I've been thinking about the crash – something just isn't sitting right about this whole thing." She shook her head. "I don't know."

Tony shrugged. "It all just sucks." He didn't seem to have thought much about the crash beyond the horror of it. "Are you and Will still planning to leave tomorrow morning?"

Arisa nodded. "If no one's here by the time we wake up." She paused and wiped a hand across her forehead. "I hope it's cooler. This is hot weather for the middle of September." Arisa got to her feet when she spotted the second group coming back.

"I can't believe you're going to leave me and Tony here, by ourselves, with all these kids and Mr. Brendan." Reese spoke up from behind Tony. Fear mixed with the frustration in her eyes and Arisa knew which was the dominant emotion.

"Do you want me to take some other kids with me?" Arisa asked, wanting to be sympathetic to the older girl's plight, but her patience with Reese's helplessness was beginning to wear thin. Her voice was edged with sarcasm. "I'm sure they'd rather go exploring than sit around here with you guys."

"No, we don't want to risk someone getting lost out there. I could just see Luke or Kris deciding they would be able to go off on their own and then get lost, or worse." Tony spoke sharply. He looked at Reese, the expression in his eyes keeping her silent. "I think Reese and I can handle it. But don't be gone too long. If you see or hear a plane, come back right away. "

"I think that's obvious." Arisa started to leave then turned back. "I really think this is a good idea. Something good is going to come out of this. I'm sure of it."

"I certainly hope so."

Arisa heard Tony mutter as she walked towards Will. She greeted him with a smile and they walked off together, gathering things they would need for their journey. They both wanted to cover as much distance as possible, which meant leaving early in the morning and getting everything together before the sun went down.

As Arisa began to pack things into one of the book bags they'd scavenged from the plan, a sudden fear rose up inside. After a moment's pause, she shrugged it away, focusing her mind instead on the task at hand. After everything that'd happened, things really couldn't get much worse.

*   *   *

It was late into Saturday night before Arisa and Will decided to set up camp. They stopped in a small clearing and looked around. The trees around them formed a canopy over their heads, letting through some of the moonlight to shine down on them, just as they had provided shade from the sweltering sun earlier in the day. A few thin clouds shadowed the dusky night sky, but the stars still shone through. Night sounds filled the air as animals woke from their daytime slumber.

Arisa struck a match from a book she'd taken from one of the plane's emergency kits. She lit the dry grass she and Will had placed under a few dried pieces of wood. The days so far had been warm, but the nights were cool enough to warrant a fire. She looked up at Will and suddenly asked. "When was the last time you had a hair cut?"

"About a month before we left. I was planning on getting it cut when we got back." Will sat down on his sleeping bag and looked at Arisa, puzzled. "Why?"

Arisa grinned. "It's kinda shaggy."

Will ran his fingers through his hair, a wry smile on his face. He pushed it back out of his eyes, the smile turning into a grimace at the gritty feel of the sun-bleached strands. It now hung past his chin, almost to his shoulders and he looked at it, the grin returning as he realized that his hair was almost as light as Candece's.

Arisa patted the French braid that kept her own hair in place. "I'd just like to be able to wash my hair some other place besides a stream. And with shampoo. Conditioner would be nice, too, but I'd be happy with any type of soap. The first thing I want to do when I get home is take a long, hot shower." She closed her eyes and stretched her arms above her head, imagining. "Then I want to sleep in my nice, comfy bed."

As Will smiled in agreement, a blanket of quiet fell. The two teens sat across from each other, watching the sparks from the fire fly up toward the night sky. Arisa looked up at the shining stars, silently making a wish. She knew it was silly but she did it anyway, taking comfort in the childish innocence. A light breeze blew through the small camp, causing the fire to flicker slightly and Arisa to shiver. A comfortable silence had settled over them. There weren't any awkward moments left since they had already seen each other at their worst. Both had already expressed amazement at how quickly the group had come together, bonding much closer in five days than many of them had during their years at school together.

"We should get some sleep." Will broke the silence.

"Right after I have prayer." Arisa bowed her head.

"May I join you?" Will came over and sat down next to her.

"Of course." Arisa waited until Will settled. Without any hesitation, she took his hands in hers and bowed her head. He followed her example joining her in silent prayer.

After several minutes of talking to God on her own, Arisa looked up. Will was still sitting with his eyes closed. She sat quietly, continuing to hold his hands until he was done with his prayer. As she watched him, she noticed, amused, his lips moved as he prayed. Her grandfather did the same thing. When he finally opened his eyes, Arisa smiled at him. He returned the smile, realizing she'd been watching him. "Ready to sleep now?"

Arisa nodded. Will released Arisa's hands and returned to his sleeping bag on the other side of the fire. Arisa unzipped her sleeping bag and crawled in as she asked him to put out the fire.

Will nodded and kicked some dirt over the small fire, smothering it. He climbed in his sleeping bag and folded his arms behind his head. He lay with his eyes open, staring at the stars and moon shining through a thin veil of clouds. He drew comfort from the knowledge that the stars he was looking at were the same he could see from outside his own home.

He heard Arisa sigh as she closed her eyes and drifted off to sleep. Will took a little longer to fall sleep, but in the end, he, too, shut his eyes and fell asleep, lulled by the whispering of the wind in the trees.

*   *   *

"Tony! Tony!" Randy shook Tony awake.

"What is it, Randy?" Tony's voice was thick with sleep. He rolled over to face Randy.

"Twila spotted a plane!" Randy's revelation caused Tony to sit straight up, completely awake. He winced as his head hit a branch sticking out of the shelter wall.

Randy continued, as Tony ruefully rubbed his head. "It was flying really low, under the clouds, right over the island! It must've spotted us because it tipped its wings! I think it went back to get help!"

"Great! Just great!" Tony muttered, his excitement dulled by the thought that immediately sprang into his mind, adding to his already throbbing head. He threw aside his sleeping bag and grabbed his T-shirt, pulling it over his head. As he stood, he hit his head again. He rubbed the bump that was beginning to form and muttered something under his breath.

"What's wrong, Tony?" Randy asked. "I thought you'd be happy we're going to get rescued. We could be home this afternoon!"

Tony looked down at Randy, a weary look coming over his features as he explained. "I am happy, Randy, but Arisa and Will aren't here. They might not have seen the plane. And, we don't know where they are, which means we can't tell them to come back."

*   *   *

"Will, wake up." Arisa shook Will.

"What?" He yawned and blinked his eyes groggily, fighting back sleep.

"We need to go." Arisa straightened up, lifted her arms over her head and then bent down to stretch her legs. She winced as screaming muscles moved. From the groan behind her, Arisa knew that Will felt the same way. They hadn't really had a chance to recover from the battering of the crash and they were pushing themselves to the limit. She looked up at the sky. A dull gray, the morning sun was barely visible behind heavy clouds that threatened rain. The depths of the woods in front of them darkened, emitting an eerie feeling.

"I think it's going to rain today." Will commented as he got to his feet. He looked uneasy. "Check out the trees. The leaves are turning so the bottoms are up. It's going to rain."

"Where'd you learn that?" Arisa was intrigued.

"My grandfather." He rolled his sleeping bag and stuffed it into the main part of his backpack. Reaching into a front pocket, he pulled out an apple and tossed it to Arisa. He took another one for himself, wiping it on his tattered shirt more out of habit than out of need. If anything, the fruit was cleaner than his shirt.

"Thanks, but I'll have one later. I didn't bring that many." Arisa threw the apple back to Will, rolled up her own sleeping bag and stuffed it into her pack. Will gave her a questioning look as he returned the apple to his bag and she quickly answered his unasked query. "I didn't want to take too many apples from the others. I don't eat much, anyway."

"Are you sure?" Will asked, concern in his voice. He gave Arisa a worried look.

"Positive. I'll eat later. Come on." Arisa picked up her pack and slipped one of the straps onto her shoulder. She kicked some sand and dirt onto the ashes from the fire while Will ate his apple, core and all.

"Ready to go?" Will swung his bag over his shoulder.

Arisa saw him wince as the straps rubbed the red welts across his shoulders. His t-shirt had become little more than rags, offering little protection for his shoulders or back. He didn't complain though. He flexed his injured arm, making sure he hadn't bumped it. Arisa had helped him take off the bandage the day before. The wound was raw but had begun to heal. He'd taken extra care to shield his arm from anything that could reopen the injury.

"Ready when you are." Arisa's voice was tired but determined.

"Okay, which way do you want to go?" Will fell in step beside Arisa.

"Let's keep heading into the woods instead of back towards the beach. If it starts to rain, the trees will at least give us some shelter." Arisa reasoned.

They walked in silence, eyes taking in every detail of their surroundings. As they went deeper into the woods, Arisa noted which direction they were going, not wanting to get lost while trying to return to their friends. There would be no way for Tony to know which way to go after them and adding lost again to their current situation would be horrible.

After few hours had passed, Arisa suddenly stopped. She dropped her pack on the ground and sat, leaning against a tree and resting for a moment.

"Are you okay?" Will glanced at Arisa.

"Fine." Arisa muttered. Her face was pale and her hands shook as she moved to pick up her bag, determined to keep going.

"Why don't we stop here so you can eat?" Will dropped his pack to the ground, opened the front pocket, pulled out an apple and bit into it as he plopped down on the ground, leaving no room for argument.

Arisa glared at him but didn't say anything. He tossed her the remaining fruit. She caught it and bowed her head to pray. A moment later, she opened her eyes and bit through the taut red skin. She looked up at the gray sky through the thick treetops. "It looks like it's going to storm. We've got to find some shelter."

"Where are we going to find shelter on a desert island?"

"Don't worry, we'll find something." Arisa replied with more confidence than she felt. She scowled as she realized how often she'd been forced to do that; to say something she wasn't sure she believed. She stood and swung her pack over her shoulder. She felt better after eating, even though she was still a little shaky. She knew that wouldn't completely go away until she got home. The past few days had been full of heavy physical work and not much food, taking its toll on all of the kids. The counselors were affected more than the students were because they gave the majority of the food and the lighter work to the younger kids.

Will stood up with a tired sigh. He picked up his bag and began to walk. Arisa fell in step beside him, pushing aside branches and stepping over logs to clear their path. They kept their eyes open for anything that could pass as shelter but didn't see anything useful. The trees thinned as they approached another clearing. The menacing clouds were closer now, threatening to inundate the island with heavy rains. Arisa and Will's suspicions were confirmed as few the first drops of rain fell. They walked faster, still seeing nothing.

"Uh, Will," Arisa broke the silence as she several more drops fell onto her face.

"I know." He brushed his hair out of his face as the rain started to come down harder.

"Look! Over there!" Arisa pointed several feet away to a shadow. The rain fell steadily now, thoroughly soaking them within minutes. The downpour was heavy enough that the pair could barely see the outline of the shadow in the distance. As the rain came down in sheets, they broke into a run. Within a few moments, they reached the shadow – a log cabin. They gasped for breath as they pounded on the door, praying someone would answer.

After several minutes, they stopped, hands bruised from beating against the hard wood.

"There's no one here!" Arisa cried, a note of desperation in her voice.

Will didn't say anything. He reached for the doorknob and turned it, hoping and praying the door would open. Surprisingly, the door yielded and swung open into the cabin. After a moment of hesitation, Arisa and Will stepped inside. Catching their breath, they looked at their new surroundings.

The cabin was small and roughly built, but the walls were solid and no rain came inside. Very little light came in through the two windows but it was enough to see by. Dusty bunk beds were stacked against the far wall, similar to those at the church camp Arisa attended. An ancient-looking wardrobe sat against the right wall. Next to it was a small brick fireplace with a few pieces of wood stacked to one side. Beside the fireplace were several cardboard boxes, stacked halfway up the wall. Against the other wall stood a rusty camping stove, which might or might not still work. There were two rough wood cupboards above the stove. A fine layer of dust covered the cupboards and boxes and the air was slightly stale. Everything had an unused, forsaken feel.

"Where did all this come from?" Arisa's voice was barely above a whisper but it sounded loud in the empty cabin.

"I don't know." Will answered, looking around for signs of life in the abandoned abode.

"Hello!" Arisa called.

A clap of thunder rattled the windows in response. Arisa jumped, startled by the noise. Suddenly, she felt laughter bubbling up and clapped a hand over her mouth. Despite her effort, a chuckle escaped.

"What's so funny?" Will was puzzled.

She answered between giggles. "We must be the only people in the world who've ever found a deserted house on a deserted island."

Will stared at her for a moment and then the absurdity of the situation struck him and he began to laugh.

"Why don't we look around and see if we can find who owns this place? It's obviously here for some reason." Will suggested after he caught his breath. "Maybe they have a phone or something."

"Good idea." Arisa unbraided her hair and shook her head, water drops flying. "I want to dry off a bit first." She began to wring out her shirt and shorts as best as she could, leaving a small puddle under her feet. She slipped off her soaked shoes and socks and stepped to one side, marking the floor with wet footprints.

To one side, another puddle of water had formed as Will followed Arisa's example, wringing out his shorts and taking off his shoes and socks. He pulled his T-shirt over his head, exposing bare skin glistening with moisture. The cut on his arm had been washed clean, and the skin was starting to lose its raw, red look. Will winced as he flexed his arm, muscles still repairing themselves.

"I'm going to start a fire so our clothes can dry while we check the place out." Will tore off a piece of one of the cardboard boxes and set it next to a small stack of kindling he'd found. "Hey, look at this!" Will forgot about the fire as he pulled some clothes out of the box he'd torn. A few pairs of cutoff jean shorts, some socks and men's underwear, and a large black T-shirt were in the first box. He moved the top box to the floor and began to look through the one that had been underneath it.

"Here, you can put these on and get out of those wet

clothes." Will tossed the T-shirt, a pair of shorts and a pair of socks to Arisa. "I'll go outside and change. I shouldn't get too wet if I hurry." He looked through the boxes for another shirt to go with the shorts he held.

Arisa didn't answer while she crossed to Will's side. She opened another box and rummaged through it. "Blankets." She pulled a large blue quilt and then a smaller white quilt from the box. The quilts were old and worn, but both seemed clean.

"I can use this to make a curtain so neither of us have to go back outside."

A clap of thunder emphasized her statement as picked up the blue quilt. She walked over to the bunk beds and tucked one edge of the quilt underneath the top mattress, letting the rest of the blanket fall down across the bottom bunk.

"Matches?" Will was filling the fireplace with wood and cardboard.

Arisa dug into her pack. She breathed a sigh of relief when she saw that they were still dry. "Here." She tossed them across the room.

As Arisa climbed behind the makeshift curtain, Will turned and lit the cardboard. The flames licked their way up the dried wood and the fire was crackling in a matter of minutes.

Will heard her emerge from behind the homemade curtain

and turned. The T-shirt she had on hung to her knees so only the very bottom of her shorts could be seen. The shorts were several sizes too big and she had to hold on to the waistband with her free hand as she walked. The bottoms hit her mid-calf. Her wet hair hung down her back in waves, a few strands curling around her face, framing it.

"Your turn." Arisa walked over to the fire and laid her clothes on the hearth, hoping they'd dry quickly. She shivered and then smiled as she realized she'd gotten her wish for a cooler day. Now the day was cool enough to make the fire more than a little inviting.

Will picked up a pair of shorts and walked over to the bunk beds. As he changed, Arisa took the sleeping bags out of both her and Will's packs. She groaned when she saw they were both too wet to use. She unzipped the bags and laid them out on either side of the fireplace. As she smoothed them out, something caught her eye. "Hey, Will," she called, "does the name George Reeves sound familiar?"

"I don't think so. Why?" Will replied form behind the curtain.

"His name's carved in the floor over here. I know that name." Arisa scowled. It'd come to her eventually, but it was going to drive her crazy until it did. She turned around when she heard Will speak again.

"The shorts are a little big, but it feels good to be dry again and even better to be in clean clothes." Will was grinning. He laid his shirt and shorts on the hearth next to Arisa's clothes.

Arisa watched as Will threw another chunk of wood into the fire. Will, she noticed, looked thin but was actually solidly muscled. He had taken it upon himself to cut wood with the dulled ax they'd found washed up on the shore and it had certainly helped keep him in shape. Many of the others had also been working hard enough to see physical changes as they burned more calories than they consumed. Whichever students could handle the work helped carry the wood Will split, and those that couldn't tended the fires throughout the day, hoping the smoke would alert someone to their presence. It kept them busy and, Arisa noted, hadn't seemed to hurt Will's physique at all.

Arisa blushed when she realized she'd been staring at Will. The blush deepened as she realized what she'd been thinking about him while she was staring. To keep him from seeing what she was sure was written all over her face, she walked over to the bunk bed and untucked the quilt. She returned to her place in front of the fireplace, spread the quilts on the floor and sat down. She shivered and rubbed her cold hands on her upper arms, trying to keep herself warm. Will sat next to her, wrapping his arms around his bent knees.

The fire provided only the dimmest light as the flames settled. The heavy cloud cover and thick trees made the day as dark as night. The pattering rain soothed the pair's frayed nerves and they began to relax. Arisa pulled one end of the bigger quilt around her shoulders and tucked the bottom under her legs. Will took the other end of the quilt and wrapped it around himself. He moved a little closer to Arisa to trap their body heat between the blankets.

The pair sat in silence, listening to the soothing sounds of pounding rain and crackling flames. Arisa stared into the fire, her mind transporting her back home where sitting in front of the fireplace, just spending time together, was a family thing. She felt tears stinging the backs of her eyelids as images of her family flickered through her mind's eye.

Will continued to look around, his gaze not resting on one thing for long. Although he was more comfortable with Arisa than he had been before, the realization of her immediate proximity brought a sudden tightening in his stomach. He broke the silence by asking, "are you warm enough?"

Arisa smiled as she answered. "I'm fine. You?"

"I'm okay." Will realized that his voice had cracked when

Arisa looked over at him, puzzled. He flushed and turned his eyes back to the fire.

Silence fell once more. The rain continued, an occasional thunderclap rumbling overhead. Torrents of rain were no longer pouring down, but the lightening hadn't ceased which made continuing too dangerous to consider. Both Arisa and Will both knew they couldn't risk being outside in the storm. Even if it hadn't been lightening, it would be too easy to lose their way, turn an ankle, or worse, break something on an unseen obstacle. They knew they had to get back as soon as possible, but they couldn't risk injuring themselves in the process. Common sense had to prevail over the desire to return to their friends.

"What time is it, Will?" Arisa asked.

"Almost one fifteen." Will looked at his watch. "I don't think this rain's going to let up anytime soon, so I think I'm going to get some sleep. You should too. You look like you need it." She knew that he knew she hadn't been sleeping well – neither of them had.

"Sounds like a plan." Arisa said. "Why don't we just sleep right here? Our sleeping bags are soaked and the fire's warm. Besides, these quilts are at least somewhat clean and I don't even want to think of what could be in those beds."

"Are you sure?" Will asked, grateful the fire had died down enough so Arisa couldn't see the hot red flush creeping up his neck. He knew what Arisa was saying was logical but he couldn't stop his face from turning red.

"Might as well." Arisa managed to keep her voice even. She lay down and turned on her side, her back to Will. She pulled the blankets around her, shivering.

Will stretched out behind her and pressed his back against hers, giving her some of his body heat. Will was asleep almost as soon as his eyes closed. After days of sleeping in harsh environments, this was practically plush and both kids felt as if they could finally relax.

Arisa drowsily pulled the blanket up around her chin, warm and dry at last. The rain was falling easier now and the steady sound mixed with Will's even breathing to lull Arisa into the deepest sleep she'd had since she'd left home.

Hours later, Arisa's eyes opened. She yawned and sat up, disoriented by her new-strange surroundings. The blanket fell from her shoulders and she shivered. She heard a noise and turned. She saw Will and remembered everything. Reaching out, she gently shook Will, trying to wake him but not wanting to be rough about it.

"Will, it's time to wake up." Arisa glanced down at his

watch and felt her stomach drop. "Crap!"

"What's wrong?" Will sat up.

"It's almost six thirty! We've got to leave before it gets too dark!"

Will cut her off. "It's too late."

Arisa looked at him, puzzled by his response. She followed his gaze to the window. Her mouth dropped and her eyes widened. She couldn't even see the trees around the cabin. The rain had stopped but the cloud cover must have been thick because she couldn't see any moonlight. Thunder rolled in the distance as the storm crossed the island. Occasionally, a flash of lightning briefly illuminated the outside, creating sinister shapes from the surrounding trees.

"What are we going to do?" Arisa whispered. "The others are going to be going crazy."

"I know, but there's nothing we can do. We have to wait for morning." Will rested a hand on Arisa's back. "We'll leave as soon as it's light."

Arisa knew his reasoning was logical and sighed. "You're right." After the events of the past seven days, she found it a relief to be able to simply agree. Here, with Will, she could finally relax. She didn't have to be strong for the kids or for Tony and Reese. She didn't have to watch a teacher she'd known for years lay unconscious, perhaps dying. She looked over at Will, thankful that he was the one with her at that moment.

Will didn't say anything as he walked over to the fireplace and filled it with more cardboard and wood. The fire had died down to coals while they had slept, so Will started it again. The flames took the edge off the chill that had settled in the air, making it feel a little more like September. He darted an occasional glance at Arisa, taking in the weariness on her face and the worry lines across her forehead. He scowled as he remembered the numerous times in the past few days when Arisa had shouldered the responsibility Tony had rejected. Reese's helplessness was understandable; she often seemed to be teetering on the edge of hysteria. Even he could tell she wasn't any good outside of her element. Will had tried to take some of the responsibility, but still wasn't confident enough around these people to act with total authority. But, no matter what he managed to do, he still felt it wasn't enough.

Arisa got to her feet and began to rummage through another box, not appearing to have noticed Will's attention. "Hey, look! Food!" Arisa pulled boxes and cans from the box. She dug deeper and found something that brought a smile to her face.

"What's that?" Will crossed to her side as she pulled several bottles of water from the box. He grinned and carried two of them to the blanket while Arisa brought the food. They sat facing each other, the cans and boxes between them.

Arisa bowed her head and Will joined her, taking Arisa's hands in his own. "Dear Lord, bless this food and be with us through the night. Also, God, please be with the others and help them not to worry about us. Keep us all safe and bring a rescuer to us soon. And put Your hands on Mr. Brendan and keep him safe. Be with our parents as well and give strength and comfort to them. Show them in some way that we're okay. In Jesus' name, Amen."

*　*　*

"Reese, come here a minute." Tony's voice was worried but he tried not to let it betray the panic he was feeling. He'd been on edge all day. The plane Randy had reported on never returned and then came the thunderstorm that not only worried the students but terrified everyone who realized Will and Arisa were outside in it.

"What is it?" Reese immediately moved away from where she had been talking to Twila, Candece and Ryan about their absent siblings. She'd been jumpy all day and Tony had been debating on how much to share with her. He loved his girlfriend but wasn't sure she could handle anything more. Now he didn't think he could do any more alone.

"Arisa and Will aren't back yet. I'm really worried. If something happens to them, I don't know what it'll do to these kids, especially Candece, Ryan and Twila. I don't think they could handle it if anything happened to Arisa and Will." He fell silent for a moment and then spoke so quietly that Reese almost didn't hear him. "I don't know if I could." He put his arm around Reese and pulled her to him. Her arms slid around his waist and she hugged him, giving as much comfort as she was receiving.

"Twila, Candece and Ryan were talking to me about Arisa and Will still being gone. They're really upset. I think you're right. I don't think any of them could deal if anything happened to Arisa or Will." Reese laid her head on Tony's shoulder. "I can't take this anymore, Tony. I can't stay here. We need to go. Somewhere. Anywhere but here."

"We have to stay. We have a job to do. A responsibility to these kids... and to Mr. Brendan. Besides, that plane will probably be coming back once the storm clears." Tony forced himself to speak firmly. Reese looked up at him, fear in her wide eyes. He knew she'd done as much as she could. The responsibility was back on his shoulders. "I'm sure they're okay. We're all going to be okay."

* * *

"The fire feels good." Arisa looked over at Will. Her voice was soft as she added. "Thank you."

"For what?" He asked, surprised. His eyes locked with hers.

"For everything you've done over the past couple days." She turned away from his intense gaze, heat rushing to her face.

Will didn't answer, suddenly aware of her closeness. He stared at his hands, unsure what to do next. Arisa pulled her edge of the quilt around her shoulders, shivering. Will moved closer to her to let her have more of the blanket.

He asked, "are you cold?"

"A little." Arisa admitted.

Surprising himself as much as Arisa, Will slipped his arm around Arisa's shoulders and pulled her close. "Better?" He whispered, his face barely an inch from hers. His arm dropped from her shoulders and settled around her waist. Arisa glanced down at Will's arm. She lightly touched the discolored skin around the cut on his arm.

"Much." She whispered back, sinking back against him, her still damp hair brushing against him, creating goosebumps across his chilled skin.

They sat, watching the flames flicker shadows across the walls. A strangeness crept into their silence as they realized the intimacy of their situation. Will's arm tightened around Arisa's waist. Arisa leaned into him, her head resting against his shoulder.

Arisa heard the words almost audibly. "*This one.*"

After a moment, Arisa let go of the blanket and let her hand drop, searching for Will's hand. She felt his fingers brushing against her arm. Shyly looking over at Will, Arisa smiled and threaded her fingers through his. He looked at her in surprise and then squeezed her hand, a smile spreading across his face. With his free hand, he reached out and traced outside the cut that ran down Arisa's cheek from the top of her temple to just under her lips.

Will leaned over, brushing his lips across her jawbone. He turned away, seemingly embarrassed by his actions. Arisa blushed but leaned over and kissed his cheek. The two sat still for a moment in awkward silence before they turned to face each other, both wanting to say something, but not knowing how to say it. Their eyes locked and their faces moved closer. Almost involuntarily, their eyes closed and their lips touched. They wrapped their arms around each other as the kiss became stronger, drawing comfort from their nearness. When they broke apart, Will whispered into her ear, "I'm going to take care of you. You're not alone."

"Thank you, Will. You've been the only thing getting me through this." Arisa whispered, her cheek against his shoulder. She raised her head and Will bent his head to capture her lips again. He pushed back her damp hair, tucking it behind her ear, and then cupped the side of her face.

When they drew apart, Will moved his hands across Arisa's arms, wanting to warm her. "We need to sleep." Will brushed the back of his hand across her cheek.

Arisa nodded. She stretched out, Will lying behind her. He wrapped his arm around her waist, holding her close. She lightly ran her fingers down Will's arm. Over the past few days, she had started to see Will's true character as he stayed strong through everything that happened. She hadn't entertained any romantic thoughts, but it seemed so natural, so right. She'd never thought something so sweet could come out of something as tragic as what they were going through – a true God-thing. She sighed and smiled. For the first time since the crash, she had no problem getting to sleep.

*   *   *

"Twila," Randy walked across the beach. His gaze was troubled. "Are you okay?" He sat down on the damp sand next to his friend.

"Fine." Twila's voice was muffled. She sat with her arms wrapped tightly around her knees, head buried in her arms.

Randy sat in silence for a minute, wanting to say something even though he knew that nothing would help. He looked out at the ocean and waited. The storm had churned the water into chaos, waves crashing into the shore, spraying sand and salt into the night air. The clouds were just beginning to clear, the shining stars starting to peek out of the haze.

"No, I'm not fine." Twila looked up. Her eyes were red and her face tear-streaked. In a voice filled with a mixture of pain and fear, she continued. "Arisa's gone and no one knows where she is or even if she's okay." She began to cry again. "I can't lose her, Randy. I can't. I'm so scared."

Randy hesitated for only a second before putting a comforting arm around Twila's shoulders. "It's going to be okay. The rainstorm probably just caught Will and Arisa off guard and they had to take cover. They'll be back in the morning."

"How can you be sure?" Twila asked, her voice choked with sobs and muffled as she buried her face against Randy's chest. He wrapped his other arm around her.

"God has brought us this far, hasn't He? He knows how much you, Candece and Ryan need Arisa and Will. He'll protect them." Randy was surprised at how reassuring his words were even to himself. "I'm sure of it."

Twila wiped her face with the back of her hand as she raised her head. The moonlight shone off the tear-streaks down her cheeks as she whispered, "thank you."

"Hey, what are friends for?" Randy smiled as he stood and stretched out a hand. Twila took it and let Randy pull her to her feet. "Ready to head back?"

Twila nodded.

Hand in hand, the pair walked back up the beach to where the rest of their group slept. They parted in comfortable silence and settled for the night. High above, the same moon and stars shone down on the slumbering students, their lost companions and, miles away, their distraught families.

Chapter Five

"Tony, wake up." Reese's terrified voice interrupted Tony's pleasant dreams.

Tony slowly opened his eyes and saw Reese standing over him, her eyes wide and filled with terror. Her face was white and she looked like she was going to faint. His stomach dropped. "What's wrong?" He sat up and Reese put her hand on his arm. It was cold.

"Do you remember the plane we saw?" Reese's grip on Tony's arm tightened. She didn't seem to notice his wince as her nails dug into his skin.

"Yeah. What about it?" Tony asked. He was fully awake now, but just as confused as he was five minutes ago. He gently pried Reese's fingers from his arm. Five red crescent marks marred the upper part of his arm.

"It was the pilot's plane – our pilot, George Reeves. He planned on us dying in the crash, Tony. He was going to lie to our parents to get ransom money, but then he found out we were here and came after us." Reese's words tumbled out as if she couldn't stop them.

"How do you know that, Reese?" His girlfriend had been on edge for a few days now, but her current actions led him to wonder if she'd passed her breaking point.

Reese glanced behind her, answering his question with a look. As they watched, a figure stepped into the light. He held a gun in his right hand, pointed toward the two counselors. Tony's expression went from puzzlement and concern to horror to anger within a matter of seconds.

"I figured if you kids were dead and no one knew it, I could ask for ransom and jet out before anyone knew any different. I'd lay low for a little while, out of sight and then take off to some South American country or some place like that. It would have taken them months, if ever, to find the bodies. You guys landing here, doing your best to get rescued, messed up my plans. Now I have to take care of you myself. Stupid kids." George sneered at Tony.

"Sorry for the inconvenience." Tony snapped as he scrambled to his feet, hands tightening into fists. Reese stood next to her boyfriend and grabbed his wrist, digging her nails into his flesh. Tony ignored the pain and glared at the pilot.

George continued talking. "I bailed out over an island near here. You might have seen it on my map back in the plane. After the first day, my curiosity got the best of me and I just had to know if anything was left. So, I jumped into the plane I'd had on the other island and checked it out. I'd been flying around for days when I saw the raft on the island edge and figured some of you must have survived. It's just too ironic you guys landed here. I wanted to lay over here after getting my money. I even have a little cabin in the woods, stocked with food, just waiting for me but you kids spoiled all of that. I was going to take care of you all right away, but when I was in my plane, I heard some news that changed my mind. Some very rich parents are offering big money for the return of their kids." George smiled and Reese whimpered. There wasn't a shred of sanity in his mismatched eyes. Her face drained of what little color had remained and she swayed on her feet. Tony put an arm around his girlfriend to support her. "Even your school is offering a large reward. If that's how much they're willing to pay for a rescue..." He let his voice trail off with his thought left unspoken.

"So, you're going to kidnap us and ask for even more money." Tony finished George's sentence. Tony's mouth narrowed into a grim line as his anger toward the man grew.

"You've got it. I figured if your parents want you that badly now, they'd be willing to pay even more if you were in serious danger." George laughed, his shrill cackle sending chills up Tony's spine. "Now, I think you better get the kids together." Neither counselor moved so George spoke again, his tone threatening. "There's a young woman out there close enough for me to hit. If you don't get the other kids together, you'll be saying good-bye to the pretty little blond."

Tony spoke through teeth clenched with anger. "Reese, get the kids."

*   *   *

Arisa opened her eyes and immediately closed them again. A bright stream of sunlight cut across her face, hurting her eyes and making her squint as she opened them again. She stirred, trying to regain some sense of her surroundings. Her back ached from how she'd been sleeping and her left hand had fallen asleep.

"You're awake." Will stood near the window, smiling down at her. He wore his own shorts and T-shirt again. "I was going to let you sleep some more. I figured you needed it. You were killing yourself taking care of those kids."

"Thanks." Arisa smiled at Will as she sat up and stretched. "Ready to head out?"

Will nodded his head with an amused grin. "I knew you'd want to get going as soon as you woke up and yelled at me for letting you sleep in, so I have all of our stuff already packed."

"Where'd you put my clothes?" Arisa asked as she stood.

Will flushed and she suddenly realized what she'd said. Her face turned red and she laughed nervously. "You know what I mean." She quickly re-braided her hair, the heavy waves still damp from the previous day's rains.

Will laughed. "I packed them too." He handed her the bag, letting his fingers linger on hers for a second before reluctantly pulling them away.

"Thank you." Arisa repeated, slinging her bag over her shoulder. She brushed her bangs back from her eyes with an impatient gesture and took a deep breath. "Let's go."

*   *   *

"What about him?" George stopped next to Mr. Brendan, a mixture of curiosity and cruelty in his bizarre eyes.

"He's dying." Tony said bluntly. "He'll slow us down."

"Maybe I'll just be merciful." George aimed the gun at the unconscious teacher, smiling in a way that chilled Tony to the bone.

Mr. Brendan had been slipping in and out of semi-consciousness for the past few days, waking only enough to swallow what the kids gave him. Tony was honestly afraid Mr. Brendan was dying, but he still slipped between the gun and the teacher.

"And maybe you'll end up with one less hostage and one less person to help you control these kids." Tony glared up at George, gaze unwavering. "Leave him alone."

Something in Tony's eyes must have told George that he wasn't going to budge. After a moment, he nodded. "Whatever. Let's go."

Tony waited, wanting to be sure George wasn't going to change his mind. A minute passed as neither one moved. Finally, George scowled and began walking. They crossed the beach to where Reese had gathered the kids.

"Let's go. This way." George motioned with his gun. In numb shock, the students began to walk.

*   *   *

Twila and Randy hung near the back of the group, trying to think of something they could do, something to make their increasingly horrible situation somewhat better. Suddenly, Twila knelt. As Randy watched, Twila unhooked the gold chain around her neck. The heart pendant and chain had been a birthday present from Arisa. She hesitated for only a second before dropping it on the ground. If Arisa found it, Twila was sure her sister would know that something bad had happened.

"Move it!" George motioned with the gun.

Twila and Randy watched Reese walk at the front of the group with George, helping lead them into the forest. Tony stayed back, doing as George had instructed him and keeping the students from straying. George hadn't needed to inform anyone of the penalty for disobedience. Candece walked next to him, the implication clear. One wrong move and she would die.

As they walked, Reese kept looking back at where her boyfriend was walking, completely unnerved by the separation. Both Twila and Randy had noticed, with mixed relief and trepidation, that they were heading in the opposite direction Will and Arisa had taken. Both were smart enough to realize that this meant two things – and only one of them was good. The first was that Will and Arisa weren't likely to be caught by George, and would still be free to find a way to help their friends. However, this also meant that Will and Arisa might not be able to find them. They kept this in mind as they continued to leave things behind for Arisa and Will to follow.

*   *   *

Later that afternoon, Arisa and Will approached the first of the shelters. A little concerned when no one greeted them, they hurried into the deserted camp, concern quickly giving way to near panic. They ran to the empty shelters, searching for any sign of what had happened. Arisa reached Mr. Brendan first. His condition was unchanged, but could find any clue as to why he was alone.

"Nothing." Arisa's voice broke as tears welled up in her eyes. "Where could they be? They wouldn't have gone after us and left him here by himself. Something's really wrong."

"What's that?" Will saw something lying on the sand, glinting in the fading sunlight. He walked over and Arisa followed. Will picked up what had caught his eye, turned it over in his hand, and then handed it to Arisa.

"It's the necklace I gave Twila for her birthday! She always wears it, Will. The chain isn't broken so it didn't just fall off." Arisa clutched the necklace in a trembling hand. "Lord God, what happened to them?" She struggled to hold back the hot tears threatening to spill over. She'd been so sure things couldn't get worse and now she didn't think she could handle anything else.

"Hey, look!" Will noticed something else a little further up the beach and he walked over to it. It was a piece of bright red cloth, probably from a t-shirt. Before he straightened, Arisa was at his side.

"I think we know which way they went. Now, if we only knew why they went." Arisa muttered to herself. Forcing herself to turn her thoughts to Mr. Brendan, she and Will returned to the teacher's side. They managed to rouse him enough to give him water and some food. He dropped back into unconsciousness moments after they fed him. Arisa covered the teacher with a blanket and placed next to him a bottle filled with fresh water. Once she finished, she looked over at Will and he nodded.

They walked along the beach, following the trail Twila and Randy had left across the sand. When they reached the edge of the woods, they saw a slash in the bark of a large tree. A couple of feet further along inside the forest, another tree had a similar slash across its trunk.

"Twila's pocket knife. She brought it with her." Arisa brushed her fingers across the cut and then turned to search at the next marker. Will hurried after her, matching her brisk pace. They kept walking for hours, making their way from one tree to the next, all the while praying for their missing friends.

*   *   *

"Here we are." George used his gun to point out an opening in the side of the rocky hill. "Home, sweet, home." He chuckled. The echoes bounced back in haunting repetition.

"What's this?" Tammy whispered to Tommy. He shrugged and she yawned. Everyone was tired beyond the point of exhaustion.

"Inside." George ordered. He stood at the entrance to the cave, glaring at the kids as they filed past him. The look in his eyes, as much as the gun in his hand, kept everyone from even considering escape.

When Reese crawled into the hole first, panic choked her and she felt the walls closing in around her. When she didn't think she could handle her claustrophobia any longer, suddenly she found herself in what seemed to be a decent sized cavern. It was dark, but not damp or musty as she had first feared. In fact, if not for the present situation, she would have found it very nice compared to the crude shelters back on the beach.

As soon as she could, Reese moved off to the side so the others could find their way in behind her. Carefully stepping away from the entrance, she put her hands out in front of her, feeling for anything that may have been blocking her path, still wary of not being able to see her surroundings. Despite how pleasant it seemed, she was still afraid of any creepy-crawlies that might be lurking in the darkness. If something had brushed against her, she would have panicked, but she was fortunate and didn't encounter anything.

It only took a few minutes for everyone to get inside. George followed Tony into the cavern, a flashlight in his mouth and the gun in his hand. When he was able to stand, he reached into his pocket and pulled out a lighter. He handed it to Tony and motioned for him to light several candles and oil lamps scattered around the cavern. Little by little, the kids were able to see their new surroundings.

The top of the cave was low enough that George's wild hair brushed against hanging rocks and several of the taller boys could have reached up to touch the ceiling. All around the cave floor were rocks, some big enough for some of the tired students to sit on and most did just that, thankful to be off their feet. The air was stale, but it was dry and cool. And even with everyone crammed inside, they had more room than their homemade shelters. Under different circumstances, the students might have enjoyed their new surroundings.

"I see you're missing quite a few people. Some of the other older ones, right?" George narrowed his eyes as he scanned the group. His gaze came to rest on Tony. He waited for the answer.

"Several of us died in the crash." Tony replied curtly, holding George's gaze for a moment. "Thanks a lot for that." He glanced at the kids around him, hoping they would understand what he was trying to do and not contradict him. Despite their current situation, most of them had the presence of mind to let Tony do the talking and they quieted those who did open their mouths to correct the counselor's statement.

George ignored the sarcasm, so lost he was in his own musings. "Well, what they don't know won't hurt them, will it? I'll ask for the money anyway."

"You shouldn't have lied to him." Reese whispered into Tony's ear. She looked over at George to see if he was watching them; he wasn't. "If he finds out, he's going to go nuts. There's no telling what he'll do to us."

"I didn't lie." Tony corrected her with a lopsided grin. "I didn't tell him how many of the missing people died. Several is a vague term. He won't find out." He grew serious. "Anyway, I had to do it. If he knew Will and Arisa were still out there, it would hurt their chances of ever finding us."

"What makes you think that they'll find us?" Reese asked, her voice shrill. Tony gave her a sharp look, but George hadn't noticed.

"I don't know for certain they will, Reese. All we can do is pray that God gives them some sign to follow."

*   *   *

Hours passed and soon the woods were black. The sun had set long ago and no moonlight pierced through the thick canopy of trees. Despite the darkness hindering their journey, Arisa showed no signs of letting up. Finally, Will knew he was going to have to do something or she would push forward until she passed out. He stopped walking. "Arisa, you need to sleep. It's past midnight. If we're going to help them, we need to wait until morning."

"No! We have to keep looking." Arisa protested. Her voice was strained.

Will reached out and grabbed Arisa's arm, turning her around to face him. He held both of her arms and looked into her eyes. His voice was firm. "You can't find them if you fall asleep walking. And you're not going to find them if you trip on something and break your neck. Please, Arisa." He softened. He was worried that this final turn of events would completely undo her. "My family is out there too. Please rest."

"Oh, Will, I'm so scared. What could have happened to

them?" Arisa buried her face in Will's shoulder and began to cry.

Will wrapped his arms around her and held her close. He gently kissed the top of her head, whispering, "shh." He knew everything was finally catching up to her. She needed to cry almost as much as she needed to sleep. She'd been the strength for everyone much longer than any sixteen year-old should have been and she'd never broken down. "Everything's going to work out. Just have faith. We're going to find them."

Arisa looked up at Will. Her cheeks were damp with tears and her bottom lip trembled. Will took Arisa's face in his hands and bent his head, touching his lips to hers. Arisa slipped her arms around Will's neck, allowing herself to be comforted.

When they broke apart, Will gave her a half-smile and asked, "will you listen to me now?" He brushed back some hair from Arisa's face and rested his hand on her cheek.

"Okay. I'll try to sleep." Arisa agreed with a sigh. The adrenaline she'd been running on all week fell away and exhaustion slammed into her. She allowed Will to help her unroll her sleeping bag and unzip it, laying it out across the ground. Arisa sank down onto it and rolled onto her side, tucking her arm under her head as Will took out his sleeping bag as well. He unzipped it and laid it over Arisa like a blanket. He lay down next to her and wrapped his arms around her, knowing she would appreciate the comfort. Although her back was to him, Will could sense the smile of gratitude on her face. Within moments, she had fallen asleep. Will joined her only a few seconds later, completely drained.

*   *   *

"Will, time to get up." Arisa shook the young man more roughly than she had intended. She'd woken almost as soon as the sun had come up and wanted to go.

"Easy there." Will looked up at Arisa; his eyes were full of worry. He sat up and put a hand on Arisa's shoulder.

"Sorry." Arisa was immediately apologetic. She brushed hair away from Will's face and rested her hand on his cheek. "I'm just really worried."

"Me, too, Arisa. My brother and sister are out there, too." Will reminded her gently as he got to his feet. He reached out and squeezed Arisa's hand. She smiled as they began to roll up their sleeping bags.

A few minutes later, Arisa spoke. "Will?"

"Yeah?" Will didn't look as he stuffed the sleeping bag into his backpack.

"Thanks for making me stop last night." Arisa said.

"Don't mention it." Will changed the subject. "Are you hungry?" He rummaged through his bag for something to eat.

"A little." Arisa admitted. The last time either of them had eaten was back at the cabin. Neither one had wanted to waste any time heading back to the camp so they hadn't bothered to eat before leaving. And then after they'd found out that their friends were missing, they hadn't had much appetite. "I grabbed some crackers from the cabin, but that's all I have."

"That's fine. We can eat while we walk."

Arisa reached into her pack and pulled out a sleeve of crackers. She handed some to Will and took some for herself, stuffing the rest back into her bag. As they picked up Twila's trail, Will reached for Arisa's hand. She threaded her fingers through his and managed a grateful smile. She drew strength from Will as they continued in silence. She silently thanked God for him, not knowing how she would have dealt with the past week without Will's support.

They walked in silence for over two hours, eyes always roaming, searching for the next marker. Suddenly the signs disappeared. Arisa and Will stopped, carefully scanning the trees and ground, praying to find something.

"Look!" Arisa pointed to a small opening in a hill a few feet away. At the foot of the hill was a bright blue hair band. She walked over and picked it up. "It's Twila's. This must be where they are."

"If they'd decided to move the camp here after that storm went through, they would have brought Mr. Brendan with them and left someone back there for us." Will came up beside her. His voice was quiet. "I have a bad feeling about this Arisa. I don't think we should go in blind. We'd better look around for some other way in, or a way to see inside so we get an idea of what's going on."

Arisa nodded, a hard light coming into her eyes. Nothing was going to keep her from getting to her sister. And she knew, without having to look at him, Will felt the same way. Will went to look around the base of the hill while Arisa checked out the top. After about ten minutes, Arisa found something.

"Will, up here." Arisa called softly. Once he'd joined her, Arisa pulled back some of the grass from an opening in the ceiling of the cave and the pair peered inside. A horrifying sight met their eyes.

All of the students were huddled together underneath them, facing the entrance. Standing between the opening and the students was George Reeves. He was saying something and waving a gun, but Arisa and Will were too far away to make out the words. After only a moment, Arisa turned her gaze from the man to the crowd, searching for Twila, know that Will was doing the same for his brother and sister. She noted, with much relief, there were no students missing from the group. Several of them were sleeping while others sat with blank stares. Tony and Reese stood at the front of the group, between the madman and the others, trying to reason with him it seemed. Finally, she spotted the familiar faces she'd been searching for. Twila sat with Randy near the back of the group. With a sigh of relief, she saw Candece and Ryan sitting in front of Twila, apparently unharmed.

Arisa let the grasses close back over the hole and turned around to face Will. Her mind was reeling from all of the connections it had made. "George Reeves!" She whispered loudly. When she saw the blank look on Will's face, she realized he hadn't recognized the kidnapper. "The pilot who bailed on us. We saw his name in the cabin, remember? I knew I'd heard it before, I just couldn't remember where."

"He must have decided he could make a lot of money kidnapping us." Will's normally soft voice was hardened with anger. Arisa could see the muscles in his jaw clenching. "I wonder how long he's been planning something like this."

"We have to get them out." Arisa's mouth flattened into a

grim line and her eyes flashed.

"Of course we do." Will put a hand on Arisa's shoulder, squeezing her shoulder to show his support as he asked the tough question. "Now, how do we do it?"

*   *   *

"I'm scared, Reese." Candece looked up at the counselor, face pale. Candece moved closer. She'd had always been fragile, but the past few days had really been rough on her. The emotional and physical strain of the past week had proven that she was tougher than she appeared, but it was taking its toll just the same. Candece knew Tony and Reese were concerned about her, but she was too worried about her brothers – present and missing – to pay much attention to her own well-being.

"We all are, honey." Reese whispered to the younger girl, hugging her. Reese's voice was steady as she tried to comfort Candece, but worry shone in her eyes. "Don't worry. We'll be okay." She held on to Candece for a moment longer before releasing her.

Candece managed to give Reese a weak smile before moving away. She crossed over to her younger brother. He looked up at her from where he sat, hugging his knees to his chest.

"Are you okay?" Candece sat down next to him, careful to keep her own fear from showing. Ryan looked as frightened as she felt.

"Where are Will and Arisa?" Ryan spoke so softly that Candece had to lean close to hear him.

"They'll find us and rescue us." Candece wrapped her arms around her brother. With all of her heart, she wanted to believe her own desperate words. "Just have faith, Ryan."

Ryan looked up at his sister and smiled. A ray of light caught his attention and his eyes followed it for lack of anything else to do. His face lit up and his smile widened. He whispered, "Candece, look! There they are!" He had the presence of mind not to point, but gestured instead.

"Sure, Ryan." Candece smiled and shook her head in gentle amusement. She didn't really believe what he said, but more than anything she wanted to see her older brother again. Before she could talk herself out of it, she looked up. Her mouth dropped open as she saw what Ryan had seen. There, looking down at them from a hole in the roof of the cavern, were Arisa and Will, dirty, tired and anxious – and determined.

*   *   *

Arisa and Will smiled and motioned for the kids to be quiet.
Will breathed a prayer of thanks that he'd taught his brother
and sister the small bit ASL he'd learned and began to sign.
Candece indicated she remembered and watched Will's hands.
After a moment, the younger Johnsons carried out their
brother's instructions.

As Arisa and Will watched, Candece and Ryan went to each
of the students and whispered to them. The students inched
forward to give Arisa and Will enough room to safely slip
through the hole. They formed a half circle around George and
their other two counselors, clearing enough space to hide Arisa
and Will when they landed.

Arisa and Will looked over at George. He was talking to
Tony and standing at an angle where he would most likely see
them. Will got an idea and signed something to Ryan. The boy
nodded, understanding what his brother needed.

"Mr. Reeves, why are you doing this?" Ryan's voice
trembled as George looked away from Tony to glare at Ryan –
away from Arisa and Will.

"Why?" He snarled. "Because of the money, that's why! I
knew your school had a bunch of rich kids going to it and I
wanted the money! Rich people like you don't know what it's

like having to actually work for your money."

As George continued his tirade, Arisa and then Will slipped through the hole. George's voice was loud enough to cover any noise made as their feet hit the ground. Candece grabbed Ryan's wrist and the boy backed into the group. Satisfied that he had sufficiently intimidated the boy, George turned his attention back to Tony.

"What happened?" Arisa came up to her sister's side. The two girls began their own conversation in sign language, moving their hands close to their bodies to avoid George seeing them.

"What are we going to do now?" Candece signed to Will after filling him in on everything that had happened since he'd left.

"You are going to stay here and make sure Ryan's safe." Will emphasized the first word. "Tony and I will take care of this." He squeezed Candece's hand and she managed a smile.

"And me." Arisa put a hand on Will's shoulder.

"No." Will covered Arisa's hand with hers. "You and Reese are going to keep the kids safe. I don't want you to get hurt." Their eyes met. "Please." His last word was barely audible, but the pleading in his eyes said it all.

Arisa started to protest, but stopped when she saw Tony

making his way towards them. He glanced around to be sure he hadn't attracted George's attention, all the while edging his way toward his friends. Reese had stayed at the front of the group, forcing herself to watch George and not Tony. George, at least, was easy enough to watch. He'd turned his wandering attention to a small radio he was trying to get working. Every few moments, he'd let loose a string of swear words, reassuring the kids about where his attention was focused.

"So, what's your plan?" Tony sat down on a rock behind Will and Arisa. His voice was so soft Arisa and Will had to lean forward to hear him. He kept his head up, but his eyes down on his friends.

"I'm not quite sure what to do, but we can't just sit here. We have to do something."

Arisa nodded her agreement to Will's statement. The three were so intent on coming up with a plan that none of them noticed that George's expletives had tapered off.

Reese and the younger students watched helplessly as George held up the gun in warning and made his way through the crowd. He shoved the kids out of his way, and within a matter of moments, he was at the trio's side.

"Hey!" George had recognized Arisa and Will. "Don't move." He leveled his gun at the pair.

Arisa and Will stood, hands at shoulder height, palms out. Arisa kept her eyes on George as she and Will moved away from the group, hoping to distract the pilot long enough for Tony to do something. From the corner of her eye, Arisa caught a flurry of movement but she didn't dare look at what was happening since George wasn't taking his eyes off of her and Will.

Suddenly, a rock flew through the air, hitting George's left shoulder. He spun around and fired.

Arisa heard everyone scream and someone fell. She watched in frozen horror as George fired a second time, aiming for Randy who was moving toward his fallen companion, but George's shot went wild when Will knocked the older man onto the ground.

Randy cried out in pain as he fell to the ground, holding his wounded leg. Arisa saw Twila and Reese go to the young man's side while Will struggled to knock George's gun away. The other students pressed back against the walls as Arisa saw the gun fly from George's hand and forced herself to move.

George was up quicker than Will anticipated, but now the pilot was unarmed. He ran at Will, knocking him down. Using his size to his advantage, George pinned Will to the ground and beat him. Will fought back, managing several solid hits, but the older man easily outweighed Will, making fighting back almost impossible. As long as George didn't give Will the chance to get up, the young man knew he wouldn't last long. As it was, he was concentrating on blocking the worst of the blows.

A shot rang out and both fighters looked up in surprise.

Arisa pointed the gun at George. "Get up." Her eyes were cold.

The pilot obeyed, never taking his angry eyes off Arisa. When he was away from Will, Arisa walked over to the young man and stood beside him. George glared at the couple, his body tense, ready to strike if Arisa wavered.

"Tony, come here." Arisa kept her eyes on George. Tony looked up from where he was now helping Twila and Reese care for Randy. Without a word, Tony left the young man in Twila and Reese's capable hands and walked over to Arisa. She handed the gun to him and knelt beside Will, who was still lying on the ground. She drew in a sharp breath as she saw his wounds.

Will was covered with blood and dirt. He had several deep scratches on his face where George's fingernails had cut him and his right eye was already swelling shut. A few cuts across his cheek and jaw were bleeding, the blood running down his face and chest to soak into the waist of his pants. His shirt was in tatters.

Arisa helped Will sit up, shaking hands trying to be gentle as she examined him. His knuckles were swollen and bleeding. He winced as Arisa moved up his injured arm to his reopened wound. Blood ran down his arm and dripped from his fingertips. Arisa took Luke's offered shirt and rebandaged Will's arm. As soon as she finished, Will reached out and touched her face. She looked up at him.

"It's over." He ran his fingers down her cheek. "We're going to be okay."

Arisa nodded, not trusting her voice to speak.

"Randy's going to be okay." Reese stood next to them. "Tony said the bullet went straight through and he doesn't think it broke anything."

Arisa turned her attention to the rest of the group. Twila knelt next to Randy, wiping the dirt off his face and talking to him to distract him from the pain in his leg. Tammy had moved to her brother's side. Tony still stood with the gun pointed at George. The rest of the students were huddled together, some sobbing quietly, others staring in shock.

Arisa helped Will to his feet. Will winced as he straightened. She put his arm around her shoulders and wrapped her arm around his waist, ignoring the blood staining her arm and her shirt. Will leaned against the young woman, thankful for her support.

"Reese, what about Tia?" Will asked, suddenly somber.

Reese shook her head, tears filling her eyes. "Tony got to Tia as quickly as he could, but there was nothing he could do."

As Reese made her way through the group to Renae, Arisa addressed the group. "We need to go. The sooner we get out of here, the better. We need to check on Mr. Brendan and get cleaned up. Tomorrow we'll see if George brought us anything useful. Tonight, we rest."

Chapter Six

"Did you guys check out George's plane?" Will asked Arisa from where he lay on the bottom bunk. He sat up, leaning back against the wall to make room for Arisa to sit next to him. He winced as his tender back scraped against the rough cabin walls.

Arisa nodded and sighed as she settled back against the wall. "There's a radio on it, but we're not sure how to work it. And it's not like we can trust Reeves to tell us." Will reached over and took Arisa's hand. The young woman spoke a little louder as she asked, "how are you feeling, Randy?"

Randy's voice came from the top bunk. "Fine, I guess. I just wish I could get out of here. I'm getting really stir crazy." Randy paused and then continued with a catch in his voice. "All of this is like some crazy kind of nightmare. I just want to go home."

A wave of homesickness washed over all three. A groan from the makeshift bed in front of the fireplace drew their attention. Mr. Brendan's eyes opened for a moment and then shut again. The trio continued to watch him for a few minutes, hoping he'd wake again. When they'd returned to their original camp the previous night, he'd shown signs of recognition, calling Tony by name. He'd slipped back into unconsciousness shortly after, but he woke up more often now, and was more coherent each time. He still didn't know what had happened, but he seemed to understand that something wasn't quite right. Tony had reported, with obvious relief, that he thought Mr. Brendan was going to pull through.

"So is that where everyone else is?" Will broke the silence. "Trying to get that radio to work?"

Arisa nodded again. "Tony thinks he can figure it out."

* * *

"Hello! Hello! Is there anyone out there?" Tony's voice was hoarse. He'd been on the radio for hours, repeating himself as he changed frequencies. Frustrated, he slammed the receiver down. He'd been through every channel more times than he could remember. He bent his head and dug his fingers into his hair, praying that something would happen. The others sat on the ground outside the plane, sensing Tony's frustration. They exchanged worried glances, but said nothing. Candece put her arm around Ryan and Tommy reached for Tammy's hand.

Reese stood and crossed to Tony. She put a hand on his back and opened her mouth to say something.

"Hello, there! Who is this?" A male voice crackled over the

speaker. It was the first outside voice any of them had heard in what seemed like a lifetime.

"Hello?" Tony grabbed the receiver and practically shouted into it. "Hello! My name's Tony Vumeccelli and I'm stuck on this island with a whole bunch of kids, an injured teacher and a crazy man whose trying to kill us." The words spilled out of his mouth, completely out of his control. He wasn't making sense and he knew it, but he was unable to stop the flood of information.

"Who is this? Is this some kind of a prank?" The man on the other end of the radio didn't try to conceal the angry skepticism in his voice. "This isn't funny."

"No, it's not, sir. I'm very serious." Tony forced himself to slow down. "My name is Anthony Michael Vumeccelli and I was with twenty-two other students and two teachers from my school traveling to Camp Ventner last Monday when our pilot bailed and the plane crashed. Some of the students and one of the teachers are dead. Another teacher is hurt really badly. We found this island and then the pilot of our plane took us hostage, but we managed to tie him up and now we're using the radio from his plane. Call Wycliffe Christian School in Wycliffe, Ohio and you'll hear about it. I'm sure there's something on the news about a bunch of kids from a private school being missing for almost a week." Tony heard the words coming out of his mouth and realized how unbelievable his story sounded. "I swear, I'm telling the truth! Please, believe me!" He was on the verge of tears and struggled to hold them back.

"Hold on a minute. I'll be back." The desperation in Tony's voice must have convinced the doubtful listener that the story was worth checking out. The radio clicked into silence as he left Tony and the other students sitting in suspense, praying he would be back.

Twenty long minutes passed before the man returned. He sounded completely bewildered by the entire situation. "So, I, uh, guess you are telling the truth." He cleared his throat and continued. "I own a little airport just off the coast and I've been given your plotted course. A bunch of pilot buddies of mine are going to be calculating where we think you might be, but I can't promise we'll make it out there today. More likely we'll be out at daybreak. Will you be okay until then?"

The cheer that erupted from the students drowned out any response Tony tried to make. Tears streamed down their cheeks without shame as they hugged each other. They were going home.

Tony turned to Twila and shouted over the babble of excited

voices. "Go tell Arisa!" Twila ran off toward the cabin, Luke and Kris following close behind. Tony turned back to the radio, wiping the back of his hand across his eyes. "We have quite a few people who are going to need some medical attention, but we should be okay for the night. Our teacher is in pretty bad shape. Just get here as soon as you can."

"We'll do our best." The man continued. "Now, I need you to find anything you can use to signal where you are. We need something we can see from the air. We have some information to go on, and we'll do the best we can to get there quickly, but anything you can do to help will make it a whole lot easier."

"I'm sure we can think of something."

"Very good." The man replied. After a moment's pause, he spoke again, sounding slightly hesitant. "Can I ask a favor of you?"

"What is it?" Tony was puzzled by the question. He didn't think there was much more he could be doing.

"I'm a reporter and this would make a great story. I'd love to get the first edition."

Tony smiled his first fully genuine smile in over a week. "Sure."

"Thanks! This is great! Now, start at the beginning and don't leave anything out."

*   *   *

"Do you think they'll find us? Do you think they'll be able to see our signal?" Tammy asked Tony later that evening.

All of the students had gathered in George's cabin not long after they'd retrieved Mr. Brendan from the beach. Now, they sat wherever they could find space: the floor, the boxes and bunk beds. Luke and Kris sat on either side of Mr. Brendan. Tammy and Tommy sat at their teacher's feet. All four of the counselors were sitting on the bottom bunk. Tony sat next to Reese with his arm around her shoulders. She leaned her head against his chest and smiled up at him. Will sat against the wall with one of the sleeping bags behind him to cushion his sore back. He wrapped his arms around Arisa and she snuggled back against him, feeling his heart beat against her back.

"How could they miss it?" Tony squeezed Reese's shoulder. She snuggled closer to Tony, more like herself now that she knew they were close to getting home. A smile spread across her face as she relaxed against her boyfriend.

It hadn't taken the resourceful students much time to think of a way to alert the search planes to their presence. Several of the students returned to their original camp and gathered the extra clothes they had left behind. Luke, Kris and José then climbed up the trees that lined the nearby northern section of the beach and tied the clothes to the highest branches they could reach. While the boys did that, Nat and some of the others gathered wood and spelled out the word "HERE" on the beach in letters almost six feet long and a foot high.

"Did you tell them about what we did to George?" Arisa ran her fingers over Will's uninjured arm.

"Yeah. That pilot-reporter guy James asked what happened to the kidnapper." Tony smiled as he remembered the look on George's face when he had Luke and José tie the pilot to a tree with some rope they had found in his plane. George had screamed obscenities at the students until Twila gagged him with one of Luke's dirty socks. The enraged pilot was still gagged and tied to the tree. None of them cared that had begun to drizzle earlier that evening. Tony had set up a system to check on George every twenty minutes, making sure the pilot hadn't loosened his bonds and occasionally giving him water. The kids knew George was more familiar with the island than any of them and no one wanted to risk an escape and a far deadlier version of previous events.

"Did you tell him about the others?" Arisa asked Tony, keeping her voice low so the rest of the kids couldn't hear her question.

Tony nodded, his smile fading. He closed his eyes and took a deep breath before opening them again. The memory of the dead students took away the counselors' smiles and replaced them with grief.

"Are they going to tell their parents?" Will asked Tony. Reese and Arisa were the only other ones who heard the young man's softly spoken question. The other students were still excitedly discussing what they wanted to do when they got home. They'd pushed the deaths from their minds, unable to deal with any of them. The older ones knew that the reality of what had happened wouldn't fully hit them until things started to get back to normal. That's when they'd realize things weren't ever going to be 'normal' again.

"He told me that the police, or someone like that would tell all of the parents everything that happened." Arisa heard Tony's voice waver. "I'm guessing he meant those kids' parents and Mr. McNeil, too."

The four fell silent and listened to everyone else chatter as the minutes passed. Little by little, the younger students began settling down. They didn't have enough energy left to sustain their excitement very long, even though they were all ecstatic about going home. They'd had too much happen and they were all exhausted, but they wanted nothing more than to be off of the island and forced themselves to stay awake.

Knowing they needed a push, Arisa spoke up, "we should be getting to sleep. It's like Christmas, guys. It'll take tomorrow longer to get here if you try to stay awake."

Several kids murmured their agreement.

Tony added, "I hope you guys realize that we're probably not going to get a chance to sleep when we get back. Besides seeing our families, I have a feeing that the media is going to have a field day with us. James said that since he's the one who made first contact with us, everyone's been talking to him about our story. Just since this morning, he's had four television stations express interest in buying our story. Get ready for your fifteen minutes."

A ripple of laughter went around the group as they stretched out wherever they could. Within moments, most were halfway asleep.

Arisa glanced at Tony and he nodded. He gave George's gun to Will who tucked it under the mattress. He then stood and stretched before carefully making his way through the mass of students. José had chosen a spot close to the door, and he reminded Tony that he'd be ready to take second watch over George in a few hours. Earlier that evening, Will and Randy had offered, but because of their injuries, they were refused. It was only one more night, Tony reasoned with them, and he and José would do just fine. After the guys reasoned, Arisa and Twila had told Will and Randy in no uncertain terms that they would not be leaving the cabin until rescue planes came. As Tony left, the three remaining counselors stretched out the best they could on the bunk.

"Good night." Arisa said.

Will gently pressed his lips against her hair and rested his cheek on her head. "Night." She heard him whisper back.

"Good night, everyone!" Twila's tired voice still held a note of joy. "By this time tomorrow night, we'll all be home!" A few other half-awake voices expressed their happiness by some muttered comments that were lost as everyone drifted off to sleep, some in mid-sentence.

Arisa sighed, happy that their journey was almost at an end. Although she knew things would never be the same, she was looking forward to having some semblance of normalcy in her life again. She pulled Will's arms closer to her. He murmured something in his sleep.

"Lord, thank You for getting us through all of this. Thank You for not leaving us. I couldn't have survived this alone." Arisa managed to pray before she, too, fell asleep.

* * *

"Linda!"

The teacher had been trying to relax in a bubble bath when her husband came into the bathroom with the phone. She had to pull the receiver from her ear as her old friend practically shouted at her. All she could understand was that he'd said something about the students.

"What is it, Chief?" She asked. Fear gripped her heart. She wasn't sure she wanted to hear what he had to say. Her husband brought her a towel and sat on the edge of the tub, waiting with her.

"We found them and they're alive."

Mrs. McKennedy repeated the message as much for her own confirmation as for her husband's benefit. "They're alive." Her husband took her hand and squeezed it. "Oh, thank You Lord."

"There are some things you need to know." The chief continued, his voice sobering.

Mrs. McKennedy closed her eyes as her heart sank. "They're not all okay, are they?" Tears squeezed out from under her eyelids.

"No. I'm sorry. Most of them are fine, but a few didn't make it."

*   *   *

"Wake up! Planes! Wake up!" José rushed into the crowded cabin. He didn't need to shout. The words themselves were enough to energize.

Within seconds, everyone in the cabin was awake and scrambling to their feet. All of the ones who could followed José outside. They could hear the plane flying overhead, a welcomed sound of civilization. Through the purple and gold morning mist, they were soon able to see its faint outline. The kids ran toward the beach that lay just behind the cabin. Tony and Reese lead the group while Twila and Arisa stayed back with Randy and Will, both of whom were still moving slow.

By the time the sisters and their injured companions reached the beach, they could see several planes circling back over the island. The kids jumped around, shouting and waving their arms around. For several heart-stopping moments, it seemed as if they had been missed. All sound died before it reached the students' lips and they stood in silence, watching the skies for some sign of acknowledgement.

Finally, one of the planes tipped its wings and cheers erupted. The kids yelled and hugged whomever they happened to be standing near. Tony and Reese held each other tightly, arms still around each other's waists as they watched the plane circle around again, this time preparing to land.

Tears ran down Arisa's cheeks and she threw her arms around Will. "Not so hard, girl. I'm delicate." Will grinned as he tenderly brushed some hair back from Arisa's face. He wrapped his arms around her and drew her to him. He bent his head and kissed her, tasting the salt from her tears. When they broke apart, Arisa smiled up at him and then they turned to watch the other four planes land, their arms wrapped securely around each other.

"We're going home." Arisa had to speak the words aloud to assure herself they were true. Will looked down at her and she repeated her statement. "We're going home." He kissed the top of her head.

As soon as the first plane landed, Kris and Luke waded out into the water to greet the exiting pilot. The man allowed the boys to help him pull the seaplane toward the shore, an amused smile on his handsome face. Tony hurried to the water's edge; Reese clung to his hand and followed. Will and Arisa hung back, drinking in the joy of their companions and their own relief. They relinquished their leadership responsibilities willingly, ready to return to the relative ease of not being the adults in charge.

They heard the first pilot address Tony. "When the other planes get in, we'll be taking you to just to the coast so we can get your teacher to the hospital. From there, two of our larger planes will take you home. The pilot that's landing now is a cop, so he'll be taking care of George Reeves. I'll need one of you to take him to the prisoner."

"I'll do it." Luke offered, running into the water again to meet the next pilot. Many of the other kids were also knee-deep in the water, oblivious to the chilly morning air and the cold salt water soaking their clothes. All they could think of was getting home.

"Tony?" The first pilot stuck out a hand and smiled, revealing dazzlingly white teeth. A camera hung around his neck. "James Van Lauser. Nice to meet you."

"Mr. Van Lauser," Tony shook the journalist's outstretched hand.

"James, please." He didn't appear more than forty; the dimples when he smiled made him look much younger.

"James, then. Thank you." Tony's voice was sincere.

"While Officer Young is taking care of George Reeves and

the paramedics are getting Mr. Brendan, do you think I could get a picture of you kids together?" Mr. Van Lauser asked.

"Of course." Tony turned to the others. "Come on."

The students scrambled to follow Tony and Reese up the beach. While Arisa and Will watched James and their friends, one of the other pilots came up to Will, shirt in hand.

"Here."

Will smiled his thanks and Arisa helped him ease the shirt over his bruised flesh. He fumbled the buttons a few times before Arisa took over. The blue denim looked out of place next to the dirty ruins of Will's shorts.

"Arisa! Will!" Twila called from where she stood next to Randy. "Come on!"

Arisa and Will smiled and joined the rest of the group. James only took a few minutes to arrange the students exactly the way he wanted and took three pictures, just to be sure at least one would come out good. By the time he finished, Officer Young had taken George to a separate plane and paramedics had lifted Mr. Brendan onto a life flight helicopter. Everyone was ready to go.

*   *   *

Arisa stared out of the plane window, looking below her to where the plane was about to land. Hundreds of people were gathered below. Most had cameras and microphones and were fighting for the best positions. She spotted the group of waiting families standing off to one side, protected from the media by a line of police officers. The anxious parents started to move forward as the plane prepared to land. From as high up as she was, she couldn't tell which ones were hers, but she knew they were there, waiting for her and Twila. She moved to the edge of her seat, straining to see familiar faces among the sea.

The return flight had been torture for the kids who wanted nothing more than to go home. They had stopped at the coast and waited for news on Mr. Brendan while they received medical attention themselves. He would be okay, but would have to stay in the hospital for a while. He wouldn't be returning to Ohio for at least a few weeks. His wife, they'd been told, was already on her way down. They'd also watched the cops unloading George Reeves. All of them were more than happy to see him taken off the plane in handcuffs, cursing the whole way. The media had been entranced by the madman, buying the kids enough time to get back to their planes without being hounded, something they knew was going to happen when they got back to Ohio, whether they liked it or not. The pilots had already warned them that everyone wanted to see them come home. They'd hoped to buy more time by taking the smaller planes and not having to switch things around, but had no such luck. They wouldn't be getting their peace and quiet just yet.

Arisa's hands shook and she glanced over at Will. He smiled at her and took her hand in his, sharing his strength. She returned the smile and looked around at the other kids who were in the plane with her. Her gaze traveled across them again and, with a shock, she realized just how much they'd been hurt. She hadn't thought about it before. They'd all been so thankful to be alive, they hadn't noticed their injuries beyond superficial care. Now Arisa saw them as the media – as their parents – would see them.

Will had a swollen black eye, numerous cuts and bruises, and a long, vicious-looking cut down his left arm. Although the shirt hid most of the injuries on his torso, some of the scrapes left spots of blood. His right hand was stiff and swollen, hardly usable. The doctors had wrapped it while they were in Florida but he'd refused x-rays, saying that he'd go to the hospital as soon as he got home. His hair was caked with dried blood at his hairline, and what wasn't bloody was so covered in dust and dirt the color was nearly impossible to tell. Randy was just as bad. Dried blood and dirt stained his shorts and shirt. His leg was wrapped in a thick white bandage, startling against the rest of the grime-covered clothing.

All the others had various cuts, bruises and scrapes from the plane accident, leaving them a multitude of colors. Melanie's, Reba's, Renae's and Ryan's broken bones had been splinted by the doctors at the airport. The kids had refused lengthy treatment, but it hadn't been until Tony informed everyone involved that his parents were successful lawyers that the kids were given their way. Arisa grinned at the memory of Tony telling off one of the cops who was trying to force them to go to the hospital.

"Look, those doctors checked us out and said none of us are in any danger. We're tired, we're dirty, we're hurt. We're going home. If you don't like it, tough. If you try to make us go against our will, I will have your badge, and if you don't believe me, ask this young woman about just how good at their job my parents are." He had motioned to Reese. She crossed her arms over her chest and nodded, her face grim.

Arisa shook her head, bringing herself back to the present. The absurdity of it all hit her and before she could stop herself, Arisa felt laughter bubbling up. She put a hand on her mouth but couldn't contain it. Will, Luke and Kris stared, thinking that maybe the stress had finally gotten to her and she had just snapped. Arisa looked at Twila, knowing her sister would understand.

Twila began to chuckle as she explained. "It's kinda how our family deals with stuff. With stress."

Arisa nodded, now laughing hard enough that she was gasping for breath. The feeling was contagious and the boys found themselves joining in. Arisa had tears in her eyes and her stomach ached, but she felt a great weight fall from her shoulders.

"We are now landing." The pilot interrupted their levity. "Please fasten your seat-belts."

The students complied, their laughter dying down. Though they quieted, the mood had changed. As soon as the plane landed, none of them waited for the captain to okay their exit. They unbuckled their belts and hurried to the door. The other plane had landed first and was already opening the door. They watched the others pour out and make a beeline for their parents. The police allowed the parents through and the adults met their children halfway.

Finally, their own door opened and Luke, Kris and Twila ran out. Arisa hung back with Will. Randy hobbled after them, helped by his father who'd been allowed through the police line early to help his son.

"Go to your parents." Will tried to convince Arisa to go ahead but she shook her head, matching her pace with his.

Both Will's and Arisa's parents reached them before the teens had a chance to walk more than a few feet from the plane. Immediately, Mrs. McDonald grabbed her daughter and pulled the young woman to her. Arisa hugged her mother tightly, tears spilling down both of their cheeks. She looked out over her mother's shoulder. Her father stood nearby with Twila in his arms. They didn't stay apart for long, joining Arisa and Mrs. McDonald in a family hug.

Other reunions continued around the McDonalds. Luke bounced back and forth between his parents, talking and hugging at the same time. Nat was in her mother's arms crying happily. Randy and Tammy looked like their parents' embraces were cutting off their oxygen. Candece and Ryan had latched onto their parents and it was impossible to tell who wasn't letting go. Mr. and Mrs. Johnson kept pulling Will into awkward side-armed hugs around their other children.

Arisa looked over at him and their eyes locked. They smiled at each other, a silent message passing between them before they returned their attention to their parents.

"Are you okay, honey?" Mrs. McDonald let go of Arisa and

ran a hand across her daughter's uninjured cheek.

"I am now, Mom. I am now." Arisa's eyes glistened as she looked from her mother to her father.

"Are you sure?" Mrs. McDonald's eyes clouded over.

Arisa felt her mom taking in the minor cuts and scrapes as well as the fatigue and general weariness she knew could be seen in her eyes. "Positive." Arisa squeezed her mother's hand. She knew that her mom could see how much this experience had changed her. Arisa smiled, hoping to put her at ease.

Behind Mrs. McDonald, Arisa saw Will approach, wanting to speak to her before leaving, but not wanting to interrupt the tender family moment. Arisa smiled at him and reached over to take his good hand, the look her eyes assuring him that it was okay. She entwined her fingers with his and pulled him toward her parents.

"Dad, I'd like you to meet Will Johnson. Mom, you should remember him." Arisa squeezed Will's hand. "He's the one who rescued us from George Reeves. He was a hero."

Will's face turned red and he looked at the ground. "I didn't do anything special." He mumbled, embarrassed by the attention. Arisa squeezed his hand and he returned the pressure.

"Thank you for looking after my daughters." Mrs. McDonald hugged the blushing young man, making his face turn a darker shade of red. Arisa suppressed a chuckle.

"All of you kids were heroes." Mr. McDonald hugged both Will and Arisa at the same time. Tears glimmered in his eyes as he looked at his wife who now stood with her arm around Twila's shoulders. "You kids were braver than most adults would have been."

Arisa started to respond but something in the crowd caught her eye. The Burnetts and the Vumeccellis were walking toward each other, hands outstretched. Ecstatic, she hugged Will so tightly that he gasped in pain before she realized what she was doing and released him.

*　　*　　*

"Tony."

Tony looked up and saw Reese walking towards him, her parents close behind. With a shock, he realized that both of her parents were doing two things he'd never seen before. They were crying and smiling – at him.

"Tony," Mr. Burnett put out a hand. "I just wanted to thank you for taking care of my daughter." He looked a little uncomfortable, but had none of the animosity he'd expressed on previous occasions. "I guess you're not such a bad kid after all."

"Thank you sir." Tony shook Mr. Burnett's hand and managed not to stammer. When Mr. Burnett released his hand, Tony found himself being hugged by the usually proper Mrs. Burnett.

"I'm so sorry for how I've treated you, Tony. We both are." Mrs. Burnett cried.

This time, all Tony could manage to do was nod his head and return the hug. He heard his father behind him clear his throat.

"Reese, I owe you an apology." Mr. Vumeccelli gruffly said, putting out his hand. "I've been too harsh on you and Tony."

"It's okay, sir." Reese said, shaking Mr. Vumeccelli's hand. She glanced over at Tony, her eyes as wide and surprised as his.

Mrs. Vumeccelli stood behind her husband. "I'm not the hugging type, but I'll offer you my hand too."

"What happened?" Tony had to ask.

"We realized that you two were more important than anything else. You mean more to us than any petty differences we may have." Mr. Burnett told the couple who were still staring at both of their parents in total disbelief. Just as they were thinking their parents couldn't surprise them any more, Mr. Burnett turned to Tony's parents and extended his hand. His wife did the same. Both Tony and Reese watched in open-mouthed amazement as their parents shook hands.

"Well, what are we standing around here for? You kids probably want to get home and clean up. Maybe we'll all go out for steaks later this week." Mrs. Vumeccelli turned and began walking towards the car. Her husband followed after giving the Burnetts a nod.

"We'll be in the car." Mr. Burnett told his daughter.

The Burnetts also walked away, leaving Tony and Reese staring after them.

Reese found her voice first. "After this past week I never thought anything would surprise me. Even after everything we saw and everything we went through, I can truly say that I never really believed in miracles until just now."

Tony put his arm around Reese's shoulder. "I'll say an amen to that."

Chapter Seven

"For remarkable demonstrations of bravery under extraordinary circumstances, the United States of America is proud to be awarding the Medal of Courage to a group of incredible young people. Help us honor these young men and women by giving them a warm round of applause as they make their way up to the platform." The President clapped as the students made their way to the stage. The hundreds of people in the auditorium stood to their feet. Their applause was deafening.

Students and their families filled the front rows. Just behind them sat Mrs. Hernandaz and Mr. Edwards, the two teachers who had missed the trip. Mr. Brendan, who had been recognized earlier, sat with his wife and the McKennedys. The rest of the faculty and students sat further back. Outsiders had filled the rest of the auditorium to overflowing. Hundreds were waiting outside, hoping to catch glimpses of the student-celebrities.

Almost a full month had passed since the students of Wycliffe Christian School had been rescued from Reeves' island. Mr. Brendan had gotten home just a few days before and was doing quite well. He would be returning to school the following month. The students' physical wounds were well on their way to being healed, but the emotional impact of what had happened remained with them. They were not alone. Everyone in their school had been shocked by what had happened, and then were devastated when the principal called an assembly to tell the student body about the deaths of six of their classmates and one teacher. Memorial services had been held for each one, and every time, most of the student body had gone. To say that the tragedy had shaken them would have been a gross understatement.

The Survivors of Reeves' Island – as they were now known – had changed drastically in the month since they had first been introduced to the country as its newest celebrity darlings. Some of them had become much more independent as a result of their dramatic experience. Many had grown spiritually from it. All took their lives more seriously, understanding that no matter how young they were, life is precious and nothing is guaranteed. None of them were the same.

As they walked up to the platform, every one of them looked physically different from when they had first stepped off the planes. All looked healthier and their scrapes and bruises were healing nicely. The broken and cracked bones had begun to mend. Randy walked with a slight limp, but he could now walk without crutches. He'd carry that scar on his leg for life. All cuts were scarring over. Will's arm was taking longer to heal since it was much deeper and had reopened more than once, but most of the results of his fight with George had healed. The majority of Arisa's cuts and bruises had already disappeared and the cut on her cheek was healing, but it, too, would leave a scar. Lasting physical reminders of what had happened.

"It is my honor to present the Medal of Courage to the following courageous young people," the president began to read their names. "Anthony Vumeccelli; Reese Burnett; Arisa and Twila McDonald; William; Candece and Ryan Johnson; Natalie Lewis; José Hendricks; Reba and Melanie Renae Jones; Luke White; Kristopher Roberts; Tamara and Randy Smith; Tommy Martin; and Renae Morgan." As he read each name, the kids stepped forward and he pinned the gleaming silver medal on their shoulders. After all of the students had received their medals and returned to their places in line, the applause died down and the President spoke again. "Now, we would like for you all to join me in a moment of silence to remember those young people who were taken from us during that tragic ordeal. Students: Amanda Whit; Joseph Black; Rebecca Jones; Jacob McNeil; Markus Long, and Tia Morgan. And we remember a beloved fourth grade teacher, Mrs.

Jennifer Thorton-McNeil. After our moment of silence, I would like members of their families to come up and receive their medals."

The large audience fell quiet as they remembered the six students and one teacher who had died. After a minute, the President beckoned the families to come forward. Another deafening roar of applause shook the auditorium. The President shook each hand and extended condolences as he gave the medals. Silence fell again as the last family walked back to their seats. Several students on the stage wiped their eyes.

The President's eyes were wet when he spoke again. "We desire that everyone remembers the bravery of our young people, both the ones who lived and the ones who died. Remember, life is a precious thing, not to be taken for granted. Think about these young people as you go about your day. Tomorrow is not promised to you. No matter your age, your life can be taken from you in an instant. Live your life to the fullest." He paused. "At this time, I would like to award four very special medals to the young adults who cared for their charges while they were on the island, showing more love and compassion than, I daresay, most adults would have in a similar situation. They stepped up when adults could not. They placed themselves last when it came to what they anyone needed and put themselves first in the line of danger. They made sure the other students were taken care of; they fed the others while they themselves went hungry. They cared for an injured teacher, even stepping between him and their kidnapper. They placed themselves between the other students and the man who threatened their lives. They displayed a courage and bravery far beyond their years. Would Ms. Reese Burnett, Mr. Anthony Vumeccelli, Ms. Arisa McDonald, and Mr. William Johnson, please step forward? We have a very special award for you."

Faces flushed with embarrassment, the four stepped out of line and shook the President's hand.

He smiled as he handed them each an envelope. "In each one of these envelopes is a slip of paper. This paper is a government scholarship to the college of your choice whenever and wherever you desire. This scholarship will pay for your college education, including room, board, books and travel expenses for as long as you are in school and as far as you wish to go into higher education. The United States needs more people like you and we would like to help you in what little way we can by providing for your further education."

Tears welled up in Arisa's eyes and she let them flow down her cheeks unchecked as she heard the other students behind her on the stage cheering as well. Reese and Tony stood with their arms around each other, smiling happily. Will smiled shyly at Arisa and reached for her hand. Arisa took Tony's hand and the four counselors stood together as the audience continued to clap and cheer. Several minutes passed and the crowd didn't stop. Finally, the President raised his hands for silence and gave his closing address.

"Too many times in the recent past, the United States has seen young people taken from us in violent, senseless acts. Too many times, other young people perpetrate these acts. We have seen in other countries how young people are looked upon as heroes if they strap on a bomb and blow themselves up in a public place. In a time when so many young people aren't sure who they can look up to, everyone here can be proud of these young people for what they have accomplished. None of them asked to be stranded for eleven days on Reeves' Island with the only surviving adult badly injured. None of them asked to be kidnapped and held hostage by a madman. None of them asked for what happened to them. None of them did anything to deserve it. Not one of us would have thought less of them if they had just given up, saying 'I don't deserve this.' But, these young people did not give up. They did not sit idly by and let things happen. They stood up and said, 'We will not die out

here. We will not give up. We will prevail. We will live.'
Learn from their example. Stand up. Persevere. Make every
moment count. Make a difference. Leave your mark on the
world. They have set a standard that we as adults need to
reach."

Once the applause died down, the President thanked
everyone for coming and ended the ceremony. For almost two
hours afterwards, thousands of well-wishing strangers
subjected the kids to handshakes and hugs that never seemed to
end. Finally, someone announced that the building needed to
be cleared out and everyone began to leave, much to the relief
of the kids who were now tired of all of the attention.

From the assembly, the students and their families went to a
party in the Wycliffe Christian School gymnasium. Friends and
family crammed into the gym, filling it with heat and noise as
everyone crowded around to see and greet the kids. After an
hour more of greetings and smiles that stretched their faces and
their patience, Arisa and Will slipped out of the gym.

As soon as they got outside, they both breathed audible
sighs of relief, the cool autumn air feeling good against their
faces. Hand in hand, they walked behind the gym, through the
soccer field and into the small wooded area behind the school.

"You know, I really didn't expect so much attention. I

mean, all of those television interviews. Then, the movie and book offers. We don't deserve all of this." Arisa unconsciously rubbed the scar on her cheek, wincing under her breath as she touched a sore spot. The doctors said she'd cut a nerve and it may or may not heal. She pulled her windbreaker close as a breeze blew by. Her free hand slipped into her pocket and felt the corners of two pictures. Twila's and Mr. Van Lauser's pictures.

Because Twila had forgotten her camera before the trip began, her picture was the last one taken of some of their group. Both pictures had been copied and the copies distributed to the survivors. Most of the kids were appreciative of the gifts, seeing the pictures as reminders of those who died. Arisa pulled her hand from her pocket. Someday, she was sure, they would be precious to her, but now all they brought to her was a rush of sadness and a wish that she could go back to the moment captured in Twila's picture and stop the students from leaving, preventing the second one from ever being taken.

Will's voice brought her back to the present. "I know what you mean." He watched Arisa out of the corner of his eye. "All we did was crash into the ocean, get nineteen kids and an injured adult safely to an island only to discover it's deserted, keep the kids and adult fed, healthy and alive for eleven days, during which we stop a mad man from killing everyone and then get us all home. It was a piece of cake. Happens of all the time."

"Sure it does." A shadow passed across Arisa's. Her eyes filled with tears and she impatiently brushed them away with the back of her hand. She hated crying. It seemed like since they'd gotten back, she'd be fine for days at a time and then something would prompt a memory and she'd spend the next hour with red eyes.

"We went through a lot, didn't we?" Will's voice was soft. He stopped and tucked some hair behind Arisa's ear. He brushed a hand across her cheek before dropping the hand back to his side.

"We did." Arisa replied with a sigh, beginning to walk again. Will fell in step beside her. After a moment, Arisa spoke again. "Did you know Reese's parents apologized to Tony for the way they'd treated him before?"

"Really?" Will was interested. "I'd heard her parents didn't like Tony because his parents brought some lawsuits against the hospital where the Burnetts worked, but I didn't know they'd treated him bad."

Arisa nodded. "Mr. Burnett actually invited some of his friends' sons to his house when he knew Tony would be there to make him think Reese was seeing other guys. Both sets of parents tried to break Tony and Reese up."

Will shook his head in disbelief. "Isn't it amazing how God uses something like what happened to us to bring people together? It's true that He uses stuff that's bad to make something good."

Arisa nodded as she answered. "My mom told me the Burnetts and the Vumeccellis prayed together when they found out what had happened. At the airport, all four of them apologized to Tony and Reese. I guess they went out to dinner the week after we got back. First time both families had been in one room at the same time."

They fell silent as they walked back through the empty playground. Brightly colored leaves crunched under their feet as they walked side by side. October was just beginning to hint at the cold Ohio winter that would be coming soon.

"It's going to be really hard to go back to school again, isn't it?" Arisa stopped and looked up at Will. She bit her bottom lip and looked down at the ground. Will reached out, cupping her chin and raising her face so her eyes met his.

"Yeah, it's going to be strange going back and trying to act like nothing's changed when everywhere we look we're going to see the kids who are missing. Even me and I hadn't known them long." Will agreed. He paused and then continued. "I don't think any of us will ever be the same again. I think we all lost and gained a whole lot when we were forced to quit being kids and start acting like adults and I don't think we're ever going to get it back."

Arisa paused, thinking about Will's statement. She nodded in agreement. "I'm glad our parents haven't made us go back yet. I think some of the kids are going to think we're stuck up because of all of the attention we've gotten. Or they're going to try to get in good with us to get on television. I know that's happened to some of the others."

"I've gotten over five hundred letters from people promising me things if I can get them in a movie audition or some other stuff like that." Will said. "I even had a few girls propose to me. I told them I'd think about it." He teased, trying to lighten the mood.

Arisa pretended to punch his shoulder. She smiled weakly but knew she wasn't fooling her boyfriend.

"What's wrong?"

"All of the kids in my class were nice enough to me before, but I was never really close friends with anyone besides Tony and Cassidy. I have a few friends younger than me, like Nat, but not any of the juniors. I'm just the 'good' girl. I've done a lot of stuff for school, but I've never been very popular and now I'm going to have television crews following me around and talking to people. I'm not sure how the other kids are going to treat me. It's all going to be weird."

"It will be strange." Will agreed, reaching over and squeezing Arisa's other hand. "But, do you know what? I don't think we have to worry about little stuff like that."

Arisa didn't ask, but the question was written on her face as she looked up at Will. Her eyes met his.

"One of the things I've learned from all this, more than anything else, is that God will always be there, no matter how bleak things seem. No matter what, we'll always have Him. And each other. No matter what happens with us, I'm always going to be here for you. Got it?" A soft smile came into Will's eyes. He slipped his arms around Arisa's waist and pulled her to him. She put her arms around his neck, rising slightly on her toes to bring her face closer to his.

"Right. Him and you. I'm the luckiest girl in the world." Arisa placed a kiss on Will's cheek and then grinned. "And I'm hoping you have a similar sentiment."

Will chuckled as he drew Arisa closer to him. She looked up, losing herself in his eyes. "Definitely." Will murmured. Their lips met in a sweet and tender kiss, drawing them together as the autumn leaves danced around their feet in the brisk fall breeze.

Epilogue

One Year Later

Arisa took a deep breath as she prepared to board the plane. Her hand shook as she tucked a stray hair behind her ear.

"Nervous?" A welcomed voice spoke into her ear and she felt some of her anxiety abate.

"Aren't you?" Arisa turned to greet her boyfriend.

Will shook his head but his eyes were serious. He reached out and lightly traced the scar on Arisa's cheek – a reminder of what had happened the last time they had been on an airplane together. Arisa really didn't mind the scar. To her, it symbolized how blessed she'd been to survive the ordeal; or, at least that's what she thought most of the time. Other times, like now, it just served to remind her of how precarious life could be.

"We both agree that God wants us to go on this trip. We're going to be okay." Will took Arisa's hand in his. She nodded, still full of uncertainty. "Besides, remember what Angel said last week? That it's better to risk death knowing you're in God's plan than to lead a safe life outside His will?"

Arisa nodded. "I believe it, but I think the butterflies in my stomach are having issues."

"Come on you two. The plane's not going to wait forever."

Nineteen year-old Madison McGregor walked by, carry-on tote slung over her shoulder. Her brother Trent was two steps behind. The two looked eerily alike. If Madison cut her waist length dark hair, she and Trent could almost pass for twins despite the two-year difference in their ages.

"If it makes you feel any better, I saw the pilot and he looks sane." Will grinned.

Arisa couldn't help but return the gesture. She picked up her bag and then reached for Will's hand. He squeezed her fingers and she felt her stomach cease its flip-flops. Though she was far from enjoying the prospect of flying, she breathed a prayer of thanks as she realized that she was no longer terrified. Hand in hand, Arisa and Will followed the McGregor siblings down the corridor and onto the plane.

Arisa settled into her seat, body tense as she knew it would be through the entire flight. She held onto Will's arm, resting her cheek against his shoulder. Her fingers absently ran over the jagged scar that trailed almost the entire length of his forearm, his own souvenir from their island adventure. It had been a bad wound. The Burnetts had said that only a miracle had kept infection at bay.

"We're going to be fine." Will whispered the reassurance again. He pressed his lips to Arisa's hair and prayed aloud.

"Dear Lord, keep us safe and show us the work you want us to do. We know you have a purpose for us going to Sarajevo and we just ask that you show us what it is."

*   *   *

The group made its way through the once war-ravaged streets. Besides Zane McGregor and his two siblings, Living Water FMC had brought three other students: fifteen year-old Michael Thitis, thirteen year-old Deven Jordan and sixteen year-old Suria Hartz. None of the kids had really known each other well before signing up for the trip but their excitement had quickly brought them all together. Even Arisa and Will, members of another FM church, were readily accepted and became a common addition to the Living Waters youth group.

Zane stopped in front of a building that had definitely seen better days. Arisa studied the sign on the iron gate, but her limited language skills didn't allow her to understand the words. She was eager to know what they were going to be doing. Their original plan to work with one of the churches in Bosnia, but at the last minute, something had happened. They'd been rescheduled but didn't have any more information. They'd spent the first day in the foreign country doing some sightseeing and waiting for a phone call. Zane had gotten it early that morning but hadn't told the others any of the details.

"This is where we're going to be working. The orphanage houses anywhere from fifty to seventy-five children." Zane pushed a button next to the gate. "We're going to be cleaning, doing some minor repairs, entertaining the children, that sort of thing."

"Fifty kids live here?" Deven voiced what all of them were thinking. The house just didn't look big enough.

"Good morning." A lightly accented voice drew the attention from the building. A pleasant, but tired-looking, woman opened the gate. "Come in." Her auburn hair was lightly streaked with gray and she had laugh lines around bright blue eyes.

"I'm Zane McGregor." He put out a hand. She shook his hand as he introduced his group.

"Leann McAllister." At the curious looks, she smiled. "My parents were missionaries from Scotland. I was born here and I took over their work at the orphanage when they moved to another city." She began to walk as she talked and the group followed. "The children are just beginning their morning classes. While they are in school, you will be working on their play area. We would also like it if you all stayed for dinner so you could meet the children."

The group followed Leann into the house and down a gloomy corridor. Arisa leaned close to Will and whispered, "I hate to think of children growing up here. I mean, I know that it's better than other places or living on the street, but it doesn't really feel like a home, does it?"

"I know what you mean." Will agreed.

Leann took them down a set of stairs into the basement. Once the entire group was inside, she turned. "Here it is."

The room was dark, a single bulb casting a dim glow over the dreary room. The walls were bare stone, clean but unattractive. The floor was also bare, clean but ugly gray concrete. A few spindly wooden chairs sat along one wall. Several dingy stuffed animals sat in the chairs, stuffing poking out through worn spots or strained seams. A deflated basketball and deformed football rounded out the toys.

"I have a class waiting for me. My assistant will be down in a few moments. He can answer any questions you might have." Leann smiled and then disappeared back up the stairs.

"So..." Zane looked at Angel and she shrugged. "Where do you guys want to start?"

"There is paint for the walls." A new voice, deep and

heavily accented, came from the stairs. All eyes turned back to the stairwell. A handsome young man entered the basement. Thick black hair, dark eyes and a warm smile. "I am Peter."

"What's with the American name?" Trent wondered aloud.

"It is not American." Peter's smile disappeared. "It is from the Bible." He looked at each member of the group as he continued. "I am Leann's assistant and I will be helping you over the next sixteen days." Arisa flushed as Peter's gaze came to rest on her. His smile returned. "And now I will ask for you to tell me your names."

*   *   *

"So, how long have you worked with Leann?" Arisa found herself between Will and Peter, painting the trim while the two men did the wider area.

"My parents abandoned me shortly after my birth. Leann found me in an alley."

"I'm sorry." Arisa felt her face get hot. She hadn't meant to bring up something painful.

"Do not worry yourself." Peter turned toward Arisa and smiled. "I am not sorry for my life, why should you be?"

"So, what exactly do you do here?" Will tried to enter the

conversation.

"I do, how do you say... oh, errands. I do errands for Leann. I watch the children. Do repairs on the house." Peter returned his attention to the wall. "Anything Leann needs me to do."

"So is this what you want to do? I mean, do you see yourself here long term?" Will continued.

"I do not have much of a choice." Peter's voice was terse. "Unlike America, options are limited here."

"I didn't mean..."

"Forget it." Peter cut off Will's apology. An uneasy silence fell over the trio.

After a moment, Arisa broke it when she suddenly recalled the voicemail she'd gotten that morning. "Will, I almost forgot, I got a message from Cassidy. Sounds like some crazy stuff is going on back home."

"Everything okay?" Will's concern was evident in his voice.

"Don't know." Arisa shrugged. "The message is really short, but she didn't sound quite right."

"You are concerned for your friend." Peter drew Arisa's attention back to him. "We should pray for her. You would like that?"

"Very much." Arisa smiled.

Peter purposefully directed his statement to Arisa alone.

"Then that is what we will do when we are finished here. Now, tell me of this friend of yours."

"You guys are talking a lot over there." Zane interrupted. "Hope you're getting just as much work done."

"Of course." Out of the corner of her eye, Arisa could see Peter smirking as she responded in a cheerful voice.

Peter caught her gaze and winked. "Please, continue."

*　　*　　*

The sounds of excited child chatter faded away as the last of the orphans were tucked into bed. Arisa sat on the bed next to a small girl with big brown eyes. Arisa smiled as she remembered back to the first night. The girl had hung back at first when the orphans met Arisa's group, but Arisa had approached and soon found herself with a shadow.

Rebecca had been at the orphanage for a few years. She'd been found, wandering the streets, barefoot and mute. Unable to tell anyone her identity, Leann had spent a year looking for the girl's family but hadn't found anything. Rebecca still hadn't spoken even though her hearing was fine and doctors could find no physical reason for her silence. She stayed at the fringes of the group, but seemed at ease in the house.

Using the bit of native language Peter had taught her, Arisa spoke. "You sleep now." Arisa smoothed the hair back from Rebecca's forehead. The little girl nodded and closed her eyes, holding tightly to the stuffed bear Arisa had given her. Arisa sat for a few minutes, waiting for Rebecca's breathing to slow. Once she was sure the girl was asleep, Arisa stood and exited the room, careful not to wake the other children.

She walked out of the back door and into the cool evening. After sixteen days of hard work, the play area was finished and the group was exhausted. They would work all day and then spend the evening with the orphans, finally dropping into their beds late at night, barely awake enough to change clothes. Now, it was the last night and everyone was saying good-bye. The children would be in school when Arisa and her friends left. Only Leann and Peter would be accompanying the team to the airport.

Arisa stood outside, looking up at the stars. Tears pricked at her eyelids as she thought about the little girl she wouldn't see again.

"It will pain you to say good-bye." Peter came out of the shadows. "You will miss her."

Arisa didn't look away from the sky as Peter stepped up next to her. "Yes, I'm going to miss her, miss this place."

"Will you miss me?" Peter's voice was softer than usual.

Arisa looked at him, startled out of her reverie. "Well, yes... but not like that Peter." She tried to say it as gently as possible. She'd suspected his feelings but hadn't thought he'd say anything. Peter nodded, looking down at his hands. After a moment, his gaze returned to Arisa's face.

"I'm sorry." She said.

"You are in love with Will." It wasn't a question.

Arisa blushed but nodded. "I am."

"I hope he knows how blessed he is."

"He does." Will shut the door behind him.

Peter looked at Will and then at Arisa. "I will see you in the morning."

Arisa nodded but didn't take her eyes off of Will. The door clicked shut as Will closed the distance between them. They were alone.

"It's been a tough couple of weeks for you, hasn't it?" Will reached out a hand. "You've always had a soft spot for kids like this, like Rebecca. Seeing it firsthand has been difficult."

Arisa nodded and allowed Will to pull her to him. He wrapped his arms around her and she rested her head on his shoulder. "When I think about leaving Rebecca, it... my heart breaks, Will."

"I know." He pressed his lips to the top of her head. "And that's why Angel sent me to talk to you."

Arisa pulled back enough to look up at Will, the question in her eyes.

"She's been talking to Leann. Angel's going to adopt Rebecca."

Arisa felt her heart leap into her throat. "You're serious?"

Will grinned and tucked a strand of hair behind her ear. "I love watching your eyes light up like that." Arisa blushed. Will brushed his lips against hers. "And," his voice grew quiet, "I'm hoping they'll do it again." Will reached into his pocket and pulled out a box.

"Will?" Arisa stepped back.

Will took a deep breath and opened the box. He turned it to face Arisa. "I know we're young, but, these past days, watching you, seeing how much you love these kids, how much you love God. And then seeing Peter watching you and realizing that he saw those same things…" Color rose in Will's cheeks, but he continued. "It made me realize that I never want to worry that I might lose you."

Arisa put her hand over her open mouth. "Oh Will."

"Arisa," Will's voice shook. "Will you marry me?"

Arisa stared at him, eyes moving from the box with the ring

to his face. His face fell and she suddenly realized that she'd been quiet too long. She shook herself out of her state of shock. "Yes."

Will's face lit up. "Yes?"

Arisa threw her arms around his neck and whispered into his ear. "Yes, a thousand times, yes."

Will pulled back enough to slide the ring onto Arisa's waiting finger. He cupped her cheek and kissed her, ring box falling to the ground, forgotten. After a few minutes, they parted. Will linked his hand through Arisa's as they turned to go back into the house.

"Just one question," Arisa stopped before they went inside. Will raised an eyebrow. "Who gets to tell my dad?"

Will chuckled and opened the door. "Your dad likes me."

"Yeah, I know." Arisa squeezed Will's hand. "You're lucky."

Will's expression grew serious. "I know."

Arisa kissed his cheek. "Come on, everyone's going to be wondering where we are." She started down the hall. He smiled as he followed her.

Three Years Later

The day began as clear and warm as any October day in

northeastern Ohio. A bright blue sky had just the lightest feathering of clouds. Trees were beginning to turn and the scent of autumn hung in the air.

The pounding on the door woke Arisa from her light sleep. Before her brain had fully registered its wakefulness, the door opened and eighteen year-old Twila bounded inside. Arisa smiled as she remembered the reason for the excitement, the reason she was waking up in her bedroom rather than the half-empty campus apartment she and Will would be sharing.

"Come on, Arisa!" Twila jumped on the bed.

"You're awfully excited this morning." Arisa tried to sound grumpy, but the grin remained in place. She swung her legs over the side of the bed and stood.

"Hey, I just want the room." Twila bounced off the bed and darted from the room before Arisa could throw the pillow she'd picked up.

Arisa glanced at the clock on her headboard and stretched. She grabbed a towel and headed for the bathroom. When she returned to her room some time later, Twila was waiting. Her own hair and make-up was already flawless, out of place with her tear-away pants and sweatshirt. Arisa removed the towel on her head and tossed it into her hamper. She shook out her hair and sat on the floor, back to Twila.

"Are we going with two braids?" Twila took a comb and began to pick her way through her older sister's hair.

At Arisa's word of agreement, Twila separated the hair and started to work.

* * *

Will paced outside the door to his brother's room. Sixteen year-old Ryan was every inch the teenager when it came to valuing his sleep. Will looked at his watch again and decided that if Ryan hadn't gotten up in two minutes, he would employ more drastic measures. A cup of cold water on the feet – which usually stuck out from under the covers while Ryan's head stayed under – would do the trick.

* * *

"Stop fidgeting." Ryan whispered to the junior attendant. Eleven year-old Oliver McDonald opened his mouth to retort, but before he could, a sharp snap of the fingers came from the other side of the aisle. Mrs. McDonald shook her head ever so slightly and Oliver closed his mouth again.

No one noticed the exchange because the music had

changed and two children were making their way down the aisle. The bride's youngest sister, fourteen year-old Josie, followed nine year-old Rebecca Michaels and eight year-old Ty McDonald. Her cheeks were pink as all eyes turned towards, her but she kept her head up and her steps slow. Behind Josie was Will's sister. Seventeen year-old Candece smiled at one of the ushers before beginning her walk. Eighteen year-old Nash White had flown in from New York City for the event. He and Will knew, though Candece did not, that her upcoming graduation gift would be a ring. The Johnsons would be having another wedding in a couple years.

A sharp intake of breath from one of the groomsmen drew chuckles from the first row of guests. Twenty-one year-old Pacey Townson's face shone as his fiancée, Cassidy Chapman, followed Candece. The sapphire blue gown looked stunning on the petite young woman. Her dark eyes sought out Pacey's blue-gray ones and friends knew they were thinking ahead to December seventh – their own wedding. Behind Cassidy was a stunning young woman in a silver dress, the material shimmering under the sanctuary lights. Twenty-three year-old Eliana Sanford-Hayes smiled at her husband as she passed. They'd been married a little over a year and, the previous night, Eliana told Arisa that they would be welcoming their first child in a little over five months. After a hug of congratulations, Arisa had laughingly thanked her matron of honor for still being able to fit into her dress.

Another groomsman – Twila's eighteen year-old boyfriend, Randy – watched the young maid of honor walk down the aisle. She caught Randy's admiring stare and blushed. As she reached the front, she turned to face the back of the church and the music changed once more. The familiar march began and the guests stood.

There, at the back of the sanctuary, holding her father's arm, was Arisa. Her dress was plain enough with little decoration. A simple beaded flower design on the bottom right of the flowing skirt was all of the beadwork and lace on the gown. The cut was fashionable and flattering, but modest. Her train was long and the veil hung past the middle of her back. The fine lace covering her face, however, could not disguise her smile or her shining eyes. She and one of the ushers exchanged a smile. Twenty-one year-old Tony stood at the back of the sanctuary, hands linked with his fiancée, Reese. All three of them knew that they and Will were remembering how this had all started. With a final nod towards Tony and Reese, Arisa signaled her father that she was ready to go. She locked eyes with Will and began her walk down the aisle.

After the words of greeting, the pastor turned to Mr. McDonald and spoke. "Who gives this woman to be married to this man?"

Mr. McDonald's voice was strong though his eyes shone with tears. "Given from God to her mother and I," he took his daughter's hands and placed them into Will's waiting ones. He looked directly at the young man and said, "and we now give her to you." Will gave a slight nod and Mr. McDonald joined his wife in the seats.

When the time came for the exchange of vows, mood set by a favorite song sung by Nat, a hush fell over the crowd. Even the restless children in the audience felt the weight of the moment and paused to listen.

Arisa took a deep breath and prayed that her voice would stay steady. "My whole life, I believed that if God wanted me to be married, He would bring the right guy to me. I had a lot of people tell me that I was too picky, that I should date anyone who was a Christian, but I knew that I wanted only God's best. And then I met you. I am always amazed at how God can take something so awful and make it so good and we're a wonderful example of that. You gave me strength when I needed it. You gave me confidence to do what needed to be done. You continue to challenge me to grow in every way. You are an

awesome man of God and a continuous blessing to my life."
Her voice wobbled and she brushed a hand across her cheeks.
"I am a better person with you than I ever was without you. I
love you, Will Johnson."

The pastor turned towards Will and nodded. Will's eyes
were already shining with tears as he began. "Four years ago,
God brought my family from Colorado to Ohio. And then he
brought me to you. And, for me, it wasn't love at first sight
because I didn't need to see you to know I loved you. I've
loved you my whole life. God whispered your name into my
heart even as I took my first breath. We have been promised to
each other since before time began. You are God's gift to me
and I will love you until the day I die."

After a moment's pause, the pastor continued. "The rings,
please."

Electricity hummed through every cell of Arisa's body as
she and Will repeated the age-old traditional pair of words that
would join them forever. Everything around her dimmed as
Will released her hands and put back her veil. He placed one
hand on her waist and other on her cheek, thumb brushing her
scar. Just before his lips touched hers, she heard him whisper,
"forever." Her mouth curved into a smile against his kiss.
After almost a full minute, the sound of applause startled her

and she remembered that they weren't alone. They broke apart and turned to face the sea of faces beaming up at them.

"Friends and family," the pastor winked at Arisa as she blushed, "it is my pleasure to introduce, for the first time, Mr. and Mrs. William and Arisa McDonald."

*   *   *

Most of the guests had gone, leaving family and close friends to see off the newlyweds. Will and Arisa would be going to Toronto on their honeymoon, but they were only covering a few hours that night. They had reservations less than an hour away and would drive the remainder of the distance tomorrow. Arisa had changed out of her wedding dress and Twila had taken it, promising to put it in Arisa's bedroom until the couple returned.

"You take care." Arisa signed to her friend. Eliana and Noah would be flying back to California early the next morning. Eliana nodded and gave Arisa another hug.

"You two need to get going if you don't want to get in too late." Tony hugged Arisa and then Will. "Drive safely."

"We will." Arisa promised as she embraced Reese.

"Call when you get there." Mrs. McDonald held her

daughter close. "I know you're a married woman now, but I'll still worry."

"I'll call." Arisa smiled.

"Take care of my little girl." Mr. McDonald sounded gruff, but those around knew that it was only because he was choked up.

"Always." Will's single word brought a nod from his father-in-law.

Mrs. Johnson moved from her daughter-in-law to her son. Her eyes were red but finally dry as she reminded him to drive carefully. Mr. Johnson said nothing as he hugged Will and then Arisa. He finally had to pull his wife away, keeping one arm around her shoulders as she smiled through now tear-filled eyes.

"Thank you guys, for everything." Arisa linked hands with Will and smiled at her friends and family once more. Will echoed the sentiment and then led his bride from the reception hall and into his waiting car. The first of the stars had just begun to appear in the velvet sky as the couple drove away.

Seven Years Later

The villagers lined up outside the tent, patiently waiting for their chance to be seen by the doctors. As they stood, they watched the children of the Americans play with the native kids. As the day grew from warm to hot, two Americans emerged from the tent with buckets of water. The two smallest children, a blond girl and a younger redheaded boy, came running.

"They are yours?" A veiled woman spoke to the American woman who offered her a drink.

The American's green eyes lit up. She answered in heavily accented, but understandable, Arabic. "Tia is three years old and Kerr turned two last month."

"You speak Arabic." The woman seemed surprised.

"My husband and I learned in preparation for this trip. My name is Twila."

"Nazuri." The woman answered. "The girl over there is my daughter Dyni. She is ten."

"She is beautiful." Twila spoke sincerely.

"Your husband permits you to go about unveiled here?" Nazuri's curiosity overcame her timidity. "And with short hair?"

Twila smiled. She ran a hand through her hair, cropped short to make the transition from Northeastern Ohio to the desert easier. "Most of your neighbors do not wear veils anymore." She pointed out.

"But you wear the fish." Nazuri pointed at Twila's necklace. "Do they not also believe a woman should be covered from eyes other than her husband's? Are they not even more strict about what a woman can do? My husband says that I am lucky to not be married to one of them for they treat women as slaves."

"My faith frees women." Twila answered gently. "If you would like to know more, we will be having a meeting tonight, after the sun sets."

Nazuri's voice trembled. "If the local leaders find out, they will kill everyone there. The government might say we have religious freedom, but they do not enforce it. Local religious leaders do as they wish, especially in our little village. You could all die."

Twila's smile faded, but she didn't falter. "We know. But it is worth the risk."

"Even for your children?"

Twila looked at her son and daughter. "When they were born, my husband and I gave them back to God. Whatever His will is for their lives... Randy and I put our trust in Him; even when it might cost the lives of our children."

The American's sincerity touched her. Nazuri nodded. "Dyni and I will come if we can."

Twila smiled again. "I must give the others water, but I will look for you tonight." She turned to go.

Nazuri reached out and touched Twila's arm. "Thank you, doctor."

"Randy and I aren't doctors."

"What then?" Nazuri was puzzled.

Twila chuckled. "We make movies."

*　　*　　*

After delivering vaccines and antibiotics until the sun disappeared, the doctors and nurses set up a space in the medical tent for the promised meeting. The handpicked team mostly came from churches the Smiths attended. A doctor and nurse came from their hometown of Wycliffe, Ohio. Two others were friends from the church in Hollywood where the Smiths went when business called them to California. The other two were volunteers from a Los Angeles church.

"How many said they would come?" The youngest of the doctors, a twenty-eight year-old pediatrician, stacked the last of the boxes in a corner. She smoothed down stray hairs as she walked over to the rest of the group.

"Five women and three men." Randy answered. He picked

up his sleeping son and carried him to a blanket at the side of the tent.

"That's good." The eldest doctor, a gentleman from Ohio, sat down and wiped the sweat from his forehead. "I wasn't sure we'd get anyone the first night."

"Here they come." Twila turned to her companions, her face shining.

This trip had been Randy and Twila's dream since Twila's sister, Arisa, had come home from her own mission's trip. After their first movie broke three box office records, they decided to make their dream into a reality. They had both been twenty-three, within a few months of each other, had a daughter and were expecting another child, but they refused to let anything get in their way. They'd faced greater odds before and knew that if this was God's will, they'd find what they needed. The media hype they hadn't wanted ended up bringing the first volunteer, a nurse from LA. The rest had quickly fallen into place and now, two short years later, they were in the Middle East, ready to distribute their faith alongside the medical treatment they financed.

After ten minutes, Randy decided to begin. All five women had come, bringing six children among them, including Nazuri with Dyni. Two of the three men had come and a couple with two children of their own had heard about the meeting from Nazuri and joined her. Though fearful of her husband finding out, Nazuri seemed eager to hear what the Americans had to say.

"Good evening." Randy spoke in his shaky Arabic. "I am Randy Smith."

The fifty-something man to Randy's right used up his limited Arabic vocabulary. "Dr. Wesley Fredricks. I am blessed to be here."

"Dr. Cassidy Waters." The woman smiled to make up for her lack of words.

"Dr. James Waters." Her husband was only a few years older than her, but had already lost most of his hair. "Our children Deborah and Rocco." The ten and seven year-olds sat quietly with their parents, knowing it wasn't a time to play.

"Nurse Madison Nini." The smallest of the group, Madison was also one of the toughest, having lived in LA alone for fifteen years.

"Nurse Amberlee Chappell." The blond woman towered over the other women at almost six feet tall.

"Dr. Hakeem Caulfield." His teeth flashed brilliantly white against his dark skin. "Praise the Lord."

"My Arabic is bad, so I will now introduce my wife who is

much better and she will speak." Randy motioned to Twila who now held their slumbering oldest child. "Twila – and our daughter Tia."

Twila smiled warmly at each person before beginning. "We are all here to offer you more than medicine. We have come here to tell you about One who offers freedom beyond anything anyone can imagine. He is the One who created all of us and He loves us more than anything else. He loves each person equally, regardless of race or gender."

She spoke for almost an hour, telling the people about their Creator and His Son. About the sacrifice for sins and the promise of eternal life. When she finished, she asked if anyone had questions.

One of the children raised his hand. "If something bad happened to you, would you still believe in this God?"

Twila exchanged a look with Randy and nodded. "Yes. When Randy and I were younger, we were in a terrible accident. Several people died." She pointed to the scar on Randy's leg. "He was shot, but God protected him. We believe that it was God's will that we survived when others did not."

"How can I know this God?" Nazuri asked.

"Me too." Her daughter spoke up.

Praising the Lord in their own native tongue, the group

began to minister to their guests, using broken versions of each others' languages. They prayed together and soon the tent was filled with laughter as the new converts rejoiced. So loud were they that no one heard the approaching men until it was too late.

"What is this meeting?" An armed man shouted as he entered the tent.

"We are American doctors." Dr. Caulfield started to explain, stepping forward with palms in the air. An explosion cut off whatever he was going to say next. He looked down at the blood starting to stain his shirt and fell to his knees.

Deborah Waters was the first to scream. Kerr woke and joined in. Everything began to move in a blur of slow motion. Randy crossed the tent to pick up his son. Cassidy Waters grabbed her daughter. Two other men entered the tent. One of the village men stood. Bullets flew. People screamed. Then, it was silent as the three village leaders were the only ones left standing.

As they left, one man said to another, "burn it down. Let our people see what happens when they listen to the message of infidels."

A few seconds later, fire began to crackle and smoke seeped into the tent. From the bodies came a stifled cough. Then another from a different place. Bodies shifted and survivors emerged.

Twila pulled Tia from the rubble, unharmed. Nazuri's daughter Dyni stood up next to Tia. Both mothers had covered their daughters. Shrapnel had left numerous thin cuts all over Twila's body and a bullet had grazed her right arm, but she had survived. She didn't need to lift the hole-riddled veil to know that Nazuri had not.

"Come with me." Twila instructed Dyni. The girl nodded, still in shock.

"Twila!"

Relief flooded through her as she heard her husband's voice, followed by her baby's cry.

"Mama!"

Twila and Randy both turned and saw the children of the village couple kneeling next to their parents' bodies. Both Waters children stood behind them, bloodied, but otherwise unharmed.

"We need to leave now." One of the men from the village stood nearby, assisting one of the women who had been shot in the leg. A wound in his side bled, but he ignored it. They were the only adult survivors from their village.

"He's right." Cassidy and Nurse Chappell stood on either

side of James. "The others are dead."

Twila placed Tia on one hip and took Dyni's hand. The villagers spoke to the newly orphaned children and the group carefully made its way out the back of the tent. The killers had already vanished, knowing the military would spot the fire and come looking. The overwhelmed and battered group climbed into the medical jeep and Randy drove them away from the blaze that had been so full of life only minutes before.

*　*　*

"We need to ask all three of you one more time. Do you want to come live in the United States with Randy and I?" Twila spoke to Dyni, Nami and Maku in Arabic. They answered affirmatively in English.

"Mr. and Mrs. Smith, I hope you realize that it is only because of your fame in America that we are allowing you to take three of our children. More dirt smeared on our good name is not what we need now." The government official spoke in clipped, precise English, reflecting the cold attitude Twila and Randy had been dealing with over the past weeks as they filed for custody of the three orphans. Dyni's father had immediately disowned the girl when she publicly confessed her new faith.

"I trust that the deaths of our friends is not the publicity you are referring to." Randy's eyes flashed though his tone was mild. "Or the lack of justice in their murders. Or the news that these children have been able to claim religious asylum because their lives are in danger here."

"We restate our official position we have religious freedom and these children would be safe if they remained in their home villages." The man stiffened.

"Like our parents?" Eight year-old Maku had picked up enough English to follow the conversation. "No, sir, we go to America where we can be free to worship our God so one day we can meet our parents in heaven."

Silence fell, broken only when the overhead announcement proclaimed that their flight was boarding. The kids followed Randy and Twila, who carried their younger children. As they settled into their seats, Twila looked out at the neighboring desert. The sun cast its dying rays over the sand and as she closed her eyes, Twila could almost hear the cries in the desert. Not those of her murdered brothers and sisters who were now forever free, rather those of the lost souls, still searching for peace. She knew that, one day, she and her family would return.

Fifteen Years Later

The sun shone its warm afternoon rays down on the crowd gathered on the beach. The smaller children played at the water's edge as older siblings wandered, marveling at how their parents had survived for over a week before rescue planes had landed on this very beach. The adults in question watch in silence for the most part, their own memories almost too overwhelming to allow for speech. It had been twenty-six years since they'd first stepped foot onto the sand of this island and none of them had been back since. Now, as part of a promotion for the twenty-fifth anniversary of *Reeves' Island* – the major motion picture starring then teen sensations Rany Masterson and Talin Cain – they'd returned.

Forty-two year-old Will Johnson slid his arm around his wife's waist and pulled her close. Unconsciously, Arisa's fingers went to the faded scar Will had received all those years ago. Though her hair had darkened with age, and then began to lighten again as threads of gray and silver appeared, her eyes still blazed with the same intensity that had captured Will from the moment he'd seen her. The oldest Johnson child, Jesse, had Arisa's eyes. Their nineteen year-old daughter Leesha, recently married to the twenty year-old son of good friends Pacey and

Cassidy Townson, had inherited her mother's personality, but her appearance fit her name. More than once, Will had wondered how much his daughter and sister would have looked alike had the latter lived. David and Leesha were only a few yards away, chatting with their seldom-seen relatives. Twila and Randy were by far the busiest of the survivors, splitting their time between their Hollywood careers and their mission work in the Middle East, all the while raising their seven children. Granted, most of their adopted children were all grown and had families of their own, but Arisa still admired her sister's energy.

"Jaci looks just like you."

Arisa turned and smiled up at Tony. He motioned towards the youngest of the Smith kids. Though he and Reese had stayed in Wycliffe, they hadn't had much opportunity to see Twila and Randy's family over the past few years.

"From what I hear, she also sounds like Arisa." Will grinned. "Twila's always complaining about how often Jaci quotes her 'favorite aunt in the whole world.'"

"Uncle Tony! Aunt Reese!" The seven year-old Johnson twins, Abul and Ani, barreled across the beach to throw themselves on their surrogate aunt and uncle. Not having children of their own, Reese and Tony had become like family to the seven Johnson children and were particularly close to the pair that Arisa and Will had adopted while visiting with Twila and Randy overseas just a few years before.

"Don't let them get too dirty, Tony." Arisa knew her plea was futile, but she tried anyway. Though in his forties, Arisa still saw much of her childhood friend in Tony's sparkling eyes and mischievous grin.

As if called by the word that had always described him, Luke appeared, his own children in tow. While both Marieh and Joss looked like their mother Elle, it took Arisa just a few seconds to recognize the personality of Luke White. Not more than a foot behind Luke was, as always, Kris and his own children. The moment he released their hands, Luke's namesake and his sister Emma made a beeline for Marieh and Joss, and the foursome took off into the water.

"Elle's going to kill me." Luke sighed as the kids didn't even pause to remove their shoes.

"Where is she?" Arisa glanced around.

"Helping her friend Tex. Something about another problem with goats in Arkansas." Luke shrugged. "I didn't quite catch the whole thing." He grinned and then added, "I also probably didn't hear it right."

"Elle still doesn't like to fly, does she?" Arisa watched as her dark-haired son tried to climb onto Tony's back without any help.

Luke shook his head. "Nope. I can't get her on a plane."

"How goes the comic book business?" Tony asked, swinging Ani onto his shoulders.

"Good." Kris's hand rose to his face to push back the glasses he no longer wore. "WIT Publications just hired us to do the graphic novels for *Tru Shepard* and *The Dragon Three*."

"Adalayde and Emily will be thrilled." Arisa gestured towards two teenagers who were attempting to discreetly watch Will's nephews. Ryan's son Connor and Candece's son Nikolas were pretending not to notice the girls' attentions, but failing miserably. Arisa felt a moment of amusement at how some things never changed. "Nat tells me her girls are huge fans those books."

"Speaking of books," Luke directed his attention towards Arisa. "I hear your latest one is doing well."

"It helps when you own a bookstore."

"It also helps to be talented." Will interjected.

"Someone's a bit biased." Arisa rolled her eyes.

After a few more minutes of idle chitchat, Arisa excused herself and headed inland, stepping just inside the tree line. She leaned back against a large truck and closed her eyes. The crash of the oceans on the shore muffled the noise of people into nonsensical white noise, a rhythmic sound that didn't require any interaction on her part. Arisa opened her eyes, sensing Will before she heard him.

"Are you all right?"

He knew her so well. He always had.

Arisa shook her head. "We almost died here. Some of us did." For a moment, she saw the faces of those who had died. The teacher and her child who hadn't returned home. Those who'd been buried at sea. The one who'd made it back to Wycliffe to be laid to rest. The forever young who never had the chance to grow up, to become whatever they'd wanted to be.

Will reached for his wife, threading his fingers through hers. "But we survived. We made it." He raised their linked hands and lightly kissed the back of her hand. "Come on, let's go get the kids and go home."

Arisa leaned her head against Will's shoulder as they began walking back towards the beach. "Home sounds good." She breathed in the salty air and straightened. "Home sounds very good."

65555207R00155

Made in the USA
Lexington, KY
16 July 2017

7